THE RAJA'S LOST TREASURE

THE RAJA'S LOST TREASURE

A RICHARD HALLIBURTON ADVENTURE

BOOK 2

GARRETT DRAKE

The Raja's Lost Treasure

First Edition 2019

Published in the United States of America

Green E-Books
PO Box 140654
Boise, ID 83714

For Janel, for introducing me
to Halliburton and for our
shared wanderlust

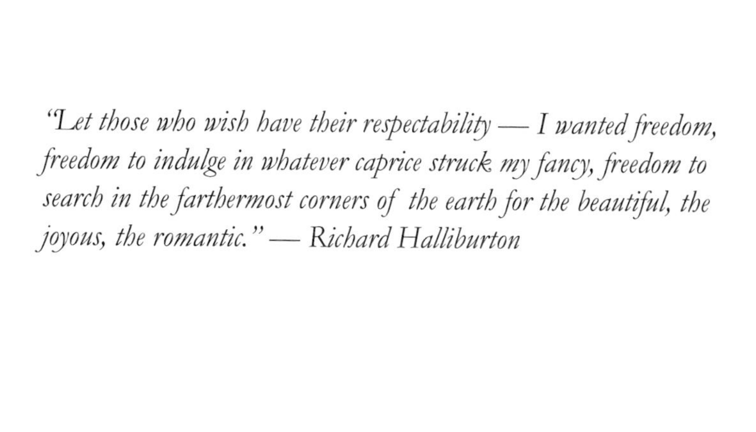

"Let those who wish have their respectability — I wanted freedom, freedom to indulge in whatever caprice struck my fancy, freedom to search in the farthermost corners of the earth for the beautiful, the joyous, the romantic." — Richard Halliburton

PROLOGUE

April 14, 1581
Kabul

MAN SINGH SIGNALED TO HIS TOP LIEUTENANT AND WAITED FOR THE SOUND OF SPLINTERING WOOD. Several soldiers clutched a battering ram as they broke into a sprint toward the palace doors. When contact was made, the door shattered and allowed Man Singh's men to stream inside. But instead of standing aside and watching the carnage unfold, Singh charged ahead, wielding his sword as an active participant in the blood letting.

Swords clashed, echoing throughout the entryway. Up and down the staircase leading to the emperor's chambers, men engaged in individual battles, almost all of them ending quickly with a body tumbling toward the ground floor. And Singh's warriors emerged victorious in the majority of the skirmishes.

When it was clear that the invaders held the upper hand, the commander of the palace guards ordered his men to stand down. They placed their weapons on the floor and surrendered.

Singh ascended the stairs to address the fallen leader.

"Coward," Singh said before driving his dagger through the man's chest.

Singh knelt next to the dying leader and wiped the

bloodied blade on his garment.

"Where is he?" Singh asked.

The man gasped as he tried to speak. After realizing he would be unable to talk, he cut his eyes toward the large doors behind him.

"Your assistance has earned you a quicker death," Singh said before slitting the man's throat. Seconds later, his body fell limp.

Singh stood and motioned for his guards to assemble near the doors. He swung them open and strode inside. Cowering in the corner was Mirza Hakim, the governor of Kabul who had been declared the emperor of the Mughal Empire. Without anyone to protect him, he shrank away, bracing for the tip of a sword to run him through.

"Stand up," Singh ordered.

"I never asked for any of this," Hakim said as he rose to his feet. "I never meant to anger Akbar. Yazdi insisted on making me Emperor."

"Silence," Singh said. "I'm not going to hurt you. I don't even care why you did what you did. Akbar will be the one to decide your fate, not me. However, there is something I need to know."

"Anything, anything," Hakim said, his face twisted with fear.

"Where is the castle's treasure?"

"I will show you," Hakim said, gesturing for Singh to follow.

Singh ordered all but one of his men, Malik, to remain in the palace, temporarily placing his lieutenant in charge.

After a short walk down the corridor, the three men descended a back stairwell and reached the castle keep several flights later.

"What do you want with this treasure?" Hakim asked.

"When Akbar arrives, it will be his anyway."

Singh shook his head. "You think Akbar will ever trust anyone in this region again, especially with his wealth? You squandered the good faith your brother-in-law bestowed upon you. And I have no doubt that you will pay a steep price for your actions."

Hakim shrugged as he flung the door open. "I never wanted this anyway."

"What?" Singh asked, eyeing his captive closely. "The treasure? The power? The influence?"

"None of it," Hakim said. "This was never going to end well, and I only went along with this coup because Yazdi didn't have the courage to declare himself the Moghul Empire's emperor. And he also believed his ploy would be a way to escape punishment if Akbar decided to crush the rebellion."

"And here we are," Singh said. "You will die for your sins against the empire. You should have let Yazdi find another pawn."

Hakim gestured for the men to proceed inside. "We all choose a path and must deal with the consequences. You seem to be choosing an interesting one right now."

Singh glared at Hakim. "If you say anything about this to Akbar, he won't believe you."

"I won't need to say a word," Hakim said. "The truth always comes out."

Singh chuckled. "Not if you bury it deep enough." He turned toward Malik. "Go get six of your most trustworthy men—men who can be bought for the right price—and transport these jewels back to the castle in Jaipur."

"You're a fool, and you're making a big mistake," Hakim said.

"The mistake would be leaving the spoils of our conquest

here and allowing Akbar to enrich himself without doing anything to squash the uprising against him. He only seeks to give me titles, but what I want are the riches that should go along with it."

"Akbar will find out one way or another."

A wry grin spread across Singh's face. "He'll have to tear my castle apart to prove such a claim. And I swear on my allegiance to the empire that he'll never find a single jewel."

Singh knelt down and scooped up the jewels, his eyes widening as he watched the glittering fortune sift through his fingers.

CHAPTER 1

April 1922
Just off the coast of Ceylon

RICHARD HALLIBURTON SHIFTED ON THE WOODEN crate as he leaned in to hear Old Ed spinning a yarn that arrested the attention of every seaman within earshot. In the distance, a storm rumbled on the starboard side, but no one seemed concerned at the moment. With all their duties completed for the day, the crew of the *Gold Shell*, a tanker bound for Calcutta, convened on the top deck to cool off as they swapped stories. Richard quickly figured out that the man known as Old Ed had long since established himself as the ship's master storyteller. And this particular anecdote he promised to be, perhaps, his best one yet.

Old Ed explained that he was once serving on a schooner from Nova Scotia with a fellow sailor named McAlister—or Mac, as Ed preferred to call his friend. One night when they were nine miles from port, reckless behavior by the captain while engaged in a race with a rival ship resulted in Mac plunging into the water after a boom hit him. Instead of stopping to save Mac, the captain cruised ahead. Left to drown, Mac defied the odds and swam to the port, reaching it without anyone's help. Mac's first order of business was to get a weapon. Once he did, he prepared for his meeting with the captain. And the next morning, Mac found the man who'd left him for dead.

"Mac walked straight up to him," Old Ed said, lowering his voice for dramatic effect, "called him a damned murderer, and right before everybody—"

A large explosion rocked the *Gold Shell.* Richard teetered on his box and tried to keep his balance before a wave of heat forced him to dive to the ground. Men all around him shouted and yelled as they scrambled back and forth across the deck. Richard's ears rang, the pressure causing a painful headache. He staggered to his feet and composed himself so he could help squelch the raging fire that had engulfed the back portion of the tanker.

A sailor clanged the fire alarm, which didn't even faze Richard.

Like that noise is going to make anyone move faster.

He turned and joined the line of men forming a bucket brigade along the starboard side of the deck. Those closest to the blaze only unshielded their faces to douse the flames lurching skyward.

Richard hustled pails along, reaching for the next one almost as soon as he let one go.

"I bet you wish you would've taken one of those fancy ships now," shouted Slim, a sailor positioned just behind Richard.

"And miss this excitement? Never," Richard replied.

Crewmen at the front yelled out directions to the men at the back, urging them to work more quickly. Richard was concerned as it was, but he soon realized that perhaps he didn't grasp just how dire the situation was based off the worried expressions worn on each sailor's face. He increased his pace to help accommodate the urgent cries near the front and said a quick prayer underneath his breath.

Richard grabbed a bucket and was in the middle of passing it when he found himself sliding backward across the deck. He crashed hard several meters away before scrambling back to his feet. When he figured out what had happened, he saw a man with a knife engaged in a fight with Slim.

Richard didn't recognize the man at first, but Old Ed had mentioned how large the crew was and it would be "damn near impossible" to learn the names of everyone aboard. However, Richard raced over to help out his friend.

Wielding his dagger, Richard sprinted straight toward the assailant and slashed at him, drawing blood on his bicep.

The man screamed out in pain before uttering a few words in a foreign language. Richard recognized it right away.

A German Reichswehr assassin.

While the German was distracted with pain, Slim delivered a few blows to the man's head before he collected his wits and re-engaged. As he studied the combat, Richard chose his moment to make another run at the German.

"I've got this," Slim said as he glanced at Richard.

Richard ignored the comment and raced toward the two men. This time, he took a flying leap, aiming for a decisive tackle. He lowered his shoulder and buried it in the German's side just above his waist. Both of them tumbled to the ground and skidded along the deck away from the fire.

As they clambered to their feet, the assassin swiped at Richard's chest. He avoided any contact but lost his balance and fell backward in the process. The German wasted no time in pouncing his target. Just as the Reichswehr soldier was about finish his assignment, Slim smacked the man in the head with a bucket. He tumbled aside, dropping his knife as he fell.

Richard seized the opportunity to reverse his fortunes and pinned the German down on the deck.

"Go ahead and finish him," Slim said.

Richard took a deep breath and prepared to plunge his knife into the man's chest when a secondary explosion rocked the ship. The German squirmed free and kicked at Richard, who stumbled but quickly regained his balance.

A big wave swept across the deck, sending several sailors sprawling, including Richard, whose dagger was swept away. The water pushed Slim to the starboard side, while the German slipped toward the edge of the port side.

Richard rushed over to help Slimas he clung to the rail with both hands.

"I'm fine," Slim said. "Go get that man before he kills one of us."

Another wave crashed into the side of the ship. Slim's left hand slipped, leaving him holding onto the vessel's railing with just his right.

Richard glanced over at the German. He was braced for another thrashing from the roiling sea.

"Go," Slim pleaded. "I can pull myself up."

Richard ignored Slim and reached down to grab his hand. However, Slim's grip gave way and he let go of the bar. Richard acted quickly enough to clamp down on Slim's wrist with both hands, securing him before he fell into the water. Slim threw his legs over the side and crashed onto the deck in a heap next to Richard.

"Nice catch," Slim said, his chest still heaving from the experience.

Richard nodded before looking across the ship toward the place where he'd last seen the German. He was gone.

Richard staggered to his feet and tried to maintain his balance as the vessel rose with another swell. He clung to a nearby ventilation tube and scanned the area. The bucket brigade had broken down, and thick black smoke billowed skyward from the stern, though the flames didn't appear to be as high. Once the *Gold Shell* received a momentary reprieve, crew members hustled to their feet to finish squelching the fire.

Richard wanted to help, but he was more concerned with finding the Reichswehr agent who had infiltrated the ship. Slim placed a hand on Richard's shoulder, making him jump. Richard spun around and prepared to take a swing when he stopped.

"You're a wee bit jumpy, aren't you?" Slim asked as he threw his hands in front of his face.

"Wouldn't you be?" Richard replied.

Slim nodded. "Given the circumstances, I probably would. But whoever that man was, he's not here now."

"We've got another week before we reach Calcutta. You think I'm gonna sleep a wink until we get there knowing that he's still on board?"

"I'll help you look for him after we get this fire out. None of this will matter if our ship goes up in flames."

Richard nodded. "You have a point. Just keep an eye out for him, will you?"

"Of course," Slim said before gesturing toward the reforming bucket brigade.

Richard stepped right back into line and continued to pass water up toward the front of the blaze, which appeared to be under control. After ten minutes, Old Ed staggered back down the line. He stopped and stared at Richard.

"Come with me," Old Ed said. "I need your help with something."

Richard remained grounded, keeping pace with the rest of the brigade.

"It wasn't a suggestion," Old Ed said.

Richard nodded and spun around to face his fellow

seaman. "What do you need?"

"We need to get something to clean up the oil on the deck. There are some sandbags below that I want you to carry up for me. My back is killing me. I think I did something to it during the explosion."

Richard followed Old Ed, talking as they went.

"Does anyone know what caused the blast?" Richard asked.

"Right now, your guess is as good as anyone's," Old Ed replied. "We can worry about what—or who—started it once we get it out. Do you have a theory?"

"I think someone sabotaged the ship," Richard said.

Old Ed froze and then turned toward Richard. "What makes you think that?"

"Have you noticed any suspicious-looking characters on board since your last stop in port?"

Old Ed threw his head back and laughed. "This is an oil tanker, kid. There's not a man aboard who doesn't seem suspicious to me in some form or another. I wouldn't trust a single one of these men to spend five minutes with my twenty-year-old daughter."

Old Ed strode toward the ladder and gestured for Richard to descend it.

"Okay, let me rephrase that then," Richard said as he climbed down. "Have you noticed anyone who looks extra suspicious?"

Old Ed hunched over, peering down the hatch with a slight smile leaking from the corners of his mouth. "Aside from you?"

"I'm serious," Richard said.

"Well, I'm probably not the best person to ask since I'm suspicious of everyone. I'd question my own mother if she were on this vessel."

Richard decided to drop his questioning since he wasn't getting anywhere with Old Ed. "Where are these sandbags?"

"Look against the far wall. They're stacked about chest high."

Richard scanned the room and spotted the pile. He hoisted a bag onto his shoulders and carried it up the ladder before slinging it onto the deck.

"Where do you want this?" he asked, his head poking up out of the hatch.

"Slide it onto this dolly for me, will ya?" Old Ed asked.

Richard positioned the sack of sand to Old Ed's liking before descending the rungs. "How many more of these do you want again?"

"At least a dozen. Just keep bringing them."

Richard turned and hustled toward the stack, but before he reached it, he was met with stiff blow to his chest that knocked him on his back. Stunned but recovering quickly, Richard scrambled to his feet. In front of him stood the German, crouched over, wielding a crowbar, and ready to swing again.

Weaponless and backed against a wall, Richard realized he needed to do something to reverse his situation and gain the upper hand.

Richard jumped back to avoid another direct blow. Then he shuffled to his left, placing his back to the large stack of sandbags.

The Reichswehr agent recoiled with his crowbar and took another wild swing at Richard, who dodged contact by ducking. The prong from the German's weapon stuck firmly in the sand. As he tried to yank free, Richard grabbed the bar with his right hand while scooping up a fistful of sand with his left. He flung the sand into his attacker's eyes, causing him to loosen his grip on the bar.

Richard kicked the man backward and took control of

the iron. The German lost his grip and fell down before scrambling to his feet. Darting up the ladder, he sought escape on the deck. But Richard was determined not to apprehend the assassin this time.

When Richard resurfaced, he found Old Ed lying on the ground and holding his head.

"Where did he go?" Richard asked as he scanned the deck.

Old Ed moaned. "He ran toward the fire."

Richard caught a glimpse of the German racing away. "Slim, Old Ed needs some help."

Slim rushed over. "What happened?"

"I got attacked again," Richard said. "I'm going after him. And this time, I'm going to finish it."

The brief respite of calm seas dissipated as the ship began to roll up and down over the waves, causing Richard's pursuit to be slowed. He staggered toward the stern where the fire appeared controlled though still burning.

Richard scanned the area and struggled to see his attacker in the glow of the flames. The sound of thundering footsteps at Richard's back arrested his attention. He turned around in time to see the German take a flying leap.

Richard didn't have time react as the force of the hit sent the two men tumbling along the deck. When they skidded to a stop, Richard rolled on top of the German and tried to use the crowbar to pin him down. But the attempt failed as the agent muscled the bar just high enough above his chest that he was able to scoot aside.

The two men wrestled for control of the weapon for several seconds, neither one of them relinquishing their grip. Richard looked into his attacker's eyes and glared.

"You started this fire, didn't you?" Richard said.

The German strained as he held fast. "You're going to die tonight."

"I don't think so," Richard said before he kicked the man's knee.

Buckling and falling to the deck, the German let go of the crowbar. Then he lunged at Richard, who jumped aside and felt the ship's railing against his back.

Richard took a swing at the German, but he grabbed the bar and managed to force it inches from Richard's throat. Resisting with all the strength he had left, Richard kneed the German, catching him by surprise. With a swift move, Richard reversed positions with his attacker and bent him over the rail.

"The Reichswehr will kill you one way or another," the German said.

"Not tonight they won't," Richard said before forcing the man overboard.

Richard watched as the agent splashed into the water and flailed around for help in the churning waves. The *Gold Shell* plowed ahead, leaving the man in her wake.

Old Ed and Slim rushed up to Richard and joined him at peering into the water.

"What was that all about?" Old Ed asked.

"Apparently, someone wants me dead," Richard said. "That was the bastard who started the fire. He was trying to create a diversion so he could kill me."

"What on Earth for?" Slim asked.

"I made enemies with the wrong people," Richard said. "But we still have a fire to put out."

"Not anymore," Slim said. "It's under control now. We just have to weather the rest of this storm, and we'll be fine."

"Well, I think you'll be safe," Old Ed said as he turned and looked at Richard. "It's a lot farther than nine miles to port."

And Richard couldn't wait to get there. His work was just beginning.

CHAPTER 2

Maredumilli, India

KARL WILHELM SCANNED THE CLEARING BELOW AS HIS elephant lumbered along the jungle path. For the first time in nearly an hour, he could see beyond the thick vegetation, though the scenery was still more lush landscape. A river sliced through the grassy area, necessitating a stop for the beasts of burden to slurp up trunks full of water.

Wilhelm eased off his seat atop the elephant and slid down the side with the help of one of their guides. He glanced at the rest of his fellow travelers as they dismounted. Hans Reinhard, Wilhelm's top lieutenant, was the first man to hit the ground and saunter over to discuss the details of their remaining journey.

"How much longer do we have before we reach this British magistrate?" Reinhard asked. "By my count, we should've been there two hours ago."

Wilhelm shrugged. "These primitive people don't understand time in the same way we do. Some of these people still hunt in the jungle for their meals. It's barbaric if you ask me, but I'm not complaining that they can be coerced into assisting us for the right price just like everybody else."

"We're going to need good help on this mission, too," Reinhard said. "We lost far too many men on the last one, strong soldiers who were caught off guard."

"I think we all underestimated Mr. Halliburton's abilities," Wilhelm said. "However, that's not a mistake we'll make again."

"I hope not," Reinhard said. "It was a costly lesson."

Wilhelm sighed and surveyed the rest of his *wolfsrudel*, his self-proclaimed wolf pack, the elite of the elite. Each one of the soldiers in his Reichswehr unit made great sacrifices to serve these missions. Germany had been crushed beneath the Treaty of Versailles's stifling sanctions, and everyone loyal to the motherland knew something had to be done. If the country's leaders allowed nature to follow its due course, Germany would lose all the power and influence it once held over the rest of the world. And that wasn't an acceptable fate for Wilhelm or any of his men.

But Reinhard had potentially sacrificed the most.

Wilhelm shoved his hand into his pocket and clasped the letter. He wanted to give it to Reinhard but couldn't. Not yet anyway.

"How are you doing?" Wilhelm asked.

"I'm fine, sir," Reinhard said, his face stoic. "Just another day serving our fine country."

"I can't help but think just how much we've all given up to embark on such a mission as this," Wilhelm said. "Especially you."

Reinhard's façade broke. His lips quivered while his eyes watered. "I'll be fine, sir. I'djust hoped I would have heard about Emilia by now."

"The doctor already told you how long she had to live."

Reinhard nodded. "I know, but it was just a guess. He said he would know more soon. But I don't know anything. And I'm afraid if anything happened to Emilia, my wife would go into labor prematurely. It makes me wonder if I'm not a complete fool for coming on this mission."

"You'd only be a fool if you weren't here. You are a man who believes in your country—and she believes in you. Besides, your wife grew up in General Hindenburg's home. You think she would really allow you to return? She's more loyal to our country than everyone in this troop combined."

"If I just knew if the doctor's timeframe was accurate, I—"

"That wouldn't change anything," Wilhelm said. "You're fighting for the future of Germany."

"But my Emilia may not even have a future, in Germany or anywhere else."

"You're carrying on because Emilia isn't your only child. And even though you haven't met your other one, what kind of world will be waiting for it? One where we are subjected to the whims of the imperialistic overlords in England and the United States? That is a fate we should fight on principle alone, whether we have children or not."

"And you think unearthing this treasure will be enough to help us get there?" Reinhard asked.

Wilhelm nodded. "It'll be a good start, though we're a long way from getting there. We're chasing a legend at this point, some fabled tale. But it's one many people believe to be true. And we won't even get a chance to do it if we don't get some help from this British magistrate."

The Reichswehr unit's guide approached Wilhelm and Reinhard. "We'll be ready to continue in five minutes."

"Thank you," Wilhelm said as he watched the man walk away.

"We should probably start loading up," Reinhard said.

Wilhelm cracked a smile. "It'll be at least ten minutes before any of these men even move a muscle toward leaving this stream. Just watch."

After a brief moment of silence, Reinhard resumed their personal conversation.

"What about you?" he asked. "Have you heard from home yet?"

"I received a note from my wife by way of a new member in our unit," Wilhelm said. "But it wasn't anything exciting."

"That's reassuring. At least they're home living their lives instead of worrying about us."

Felix Ludwig, one of the Reichswehr unit's more daring soldiers, dumped a bucket of water on his head as he approached Wilhelm and Reinhard.

"Did you forget to invite me to your meeting of the minds?" Ludwig asked, cracking a faint smile.

"We were discussing our mission," Reinhard said. "Care to contribute to how we're going to find all this treasure without getting caught and sneak it out of the country?"

Ludwig shrugged. "The sneaking it out part is easy, especially when we can press diamonds and jewels into the palms of people eager to grant us access. We'll be home in Germany before you can say *Maredumelli.* It's finding the treasure that is obviously the bigger obstacle."

"We found King Tutankhamun's tomb," Wilhelm said. "But it was securing the treasure that we struggled to do."

Ludwig wagged his finger. "That was an entirely different situation. Plus, we had no idea that we would have to do everything while fighting off another team of archeologists. We weren't prepared."

"It was *one* man," Reinhard said. "One overly zealous American."

"Yet that American managed to outwit us in the quest to take all the treasures from the king's tomb out of the Valley of the Kings," Ludwig said. "We barely even held onto the gold because of that agent. He ruined everything."

"If we see him again, I will personally see to it that *he* is the one ruined," Wilhelm said. "We haven't come this far to have our plans thwarted by a bumbling idiot who happens to be in the right place at the right time."

"I'd hardly consider him a *bumbling idiot*, sir," Reinhard said. "And it's quite possible he could be worth more to us alive than dead. After all, he is the one who knows where all that treasure is in Egypt. Maybe we could convince him to tell us where he stashed that gold mask."

Wilhelm shook his head with a sneer. "Not on my watch. He's like a wild animal that needs to be put down before he hurts someone else. No matter how harmless he looks, we all know the reality of letting him roam wild."

Ludwig nodded in agreement. "You think he's following us now?"

Wilhelm shrugged. "I've yet to hear word from the agent I assigned to Mr. Halliburton. But I can assure you that if he got on that ship to follow us here, he'll be dead by now."

"Which ship was he on?" Reinhard asked.

"The*Gold Shell*," Wilhelm said. "She's due at port in three days. We'll know soon enough."

"I hope he's dead," Ludwig said.

Wilhelm looked at his watch and nodded. "If not, I'll kill him myself."

* * *

AN HOUR LATER, the caravan lumbered into Maredumilli, a small village nestled just east of the Alluri Sitaramaraju Forest. The fact that Wilhelm and his team had to travel to such a remote area to find a helpful British magistrate spoke volumes about the enmity between Germany and their foes during the war. But Wilhelm didn't need the help of an entire legion of British officials. He just needed one. And Wilhelm found his man in Alex Fullerton.

"You finally made it," Fullerton said as he greeted Wilhelm's team.

Wilhelm slid down the side of his elephant. "It took us so long to get here that I was beginning to wonder if this village was something of a myth."

Fullerton chuckled. "This country is teeming with similar stories, but I can assure you that you have arrived at a place that exists on the map. Would you care for some tea?"

Wilhelm nodded and gestured for Reinhard to follow. The three men walked up the steps of a small wooden structure erected on stilts several feet off the ground. Fullerton opened a screen door and held it for his guests.

"I would apologize for the heat, but it's only going to get hotter in the days ahead," Fullerton said as he invited the men to sit in the chairs across from his desk.

"How can you stand to live here?" Reinhard asked.

"Someone has to keep these people in line, and I was the unfortunate one assigned to this task here," Fullerton said, settling into his seat. "It's also why I'm not so adverse to helping out a few mercenaries who want to explore the country, especially if the price is still what we agreed upon."

Wilhelm dug into his pocket and produced a wad of cash before dropping it on the Fullerton's desk. "You can look for yourself. It's all there."

Fullerton sifted briefly through the stack of bills without counting all of it, apparently satisfied that the full amount was included. He collected it and placed it into a small safe on the floor behind his desk. When he was finished, he turned around and stood, holding a handful of documents.

"I believe this is what you came for," Fullerton said

before dropping them in front of Wilhelm.

Wilhelm leaned forward in his chair and studied the papers, inspecting all the details to ensure that everything was in order. As he finished each one, he'd hand it to Reinhard to look over as well. When Wilhelm was done, he looked at his top lieutenant and nodded.

"Looks good to me," Reinhard said to Wilhelm.

Wilhelm turned to Fullerton. "In that case, I think we're ready to go."

Fullerton frowned. "But what about your tea?"

"It's too hot for tea," Wilhelm said. "Besides, we're on a tight time schedule."

"Good luck," Fullerton said with a chuckle. "This is India. The only things that move quickly around here are trains and tigers—and both of them are even known to creep on occasion."

"I'll keep that in mind," Wilhelm said as he turned toward the door.

"I'd advise you to proceed cautiously," Fullerton said. "Even with those documents, you still might attract more attention than you desire. It's not difficult to spot easy targets for the Thugs."

"I thought your government took care of them?" Wilhelm asked.

Fullerton shrugged. "The official position is that they've been more or less eradicated for lack of a better term, but let me assure you that's far from the truth. Those bandits roam hillsides all across this country in search of easy prey."

"I'm sure we can handle ourselves," Reinhard said. "This isn't a group of tourists."

"I understand that, but this is foreign soil to you, and if you don't know the safest passage through, you're leaving much to chance. Now, where are you headed next?"

"I didn't say," Wilhelm said. "It's better that way."

"I wouldn't be so sure. If you're headed north, you need a guide," Fullerton said.

Wilhelm sighed. "I will just pay these men out here to continue on."

Fullerton smiled. "Walk outside and tell them that you want them to accompany you through the Papikonda Hills directly north from here. Let's see how many takers you get."

Wilhelm narrowed his eyes as he glared at Fullerton. "You're wasting my time."

Storming out of the small building, Wilhelm whistled and signaled for his entire entourage to join him. They all hustled over, Reichswehr and guides alike.

"Gentleman," Wilhelm began, "we are about to continue the next leg of our journey through the Papikonda Hills. If you don't feel you are up to the challenge, you may—"

Before Wilhelm could finish his thought, every guide dropped his gear and walked away, turning around and not looking back. He watched them shake their heads as they scattered.

"They're just going to leave their elephants like this?" Reinhard asked as his mouth fell agape.

Fullerton sauntered up behind the remaining Reichswehr soldiers. "You can't get those elephants through the forest. The trails are too steep and narrow. You're going to need a new guide."

"And how much will one of these guides cost me?" Wilhelm asked.

"I can get you one this afternoon for a hundred pounds," Fullerton said.

Wilhelm cocked his head to one side. "A hundred pounds? Are you mad?"

Fullerton sighed. "At this point, I don't see that you have

much of a choice. Those documents aren't going to do you much good if you can't get past the next set of hills."

Wilhelm nodded to Ludwig, who darted behind Fullerton and grabbed his head before placing a knife at his neck.

"Is this really necessary?" Fullerton asked, refusing to struggle.

"You're going to get me a guide," Wilhelm said, "and you're going to do it right now."

"The only way you're going to get a guide is to pay me a hundred pounds," Fullerton said. "And if you kill me anyway, the moment you get into any trouble, it'll be obvious what happened to even the dimmest government official."

Ludwig removed the knife from Fullerton's neck and shoved him in the back.

"Now, if you'll hand over my fee, I'll go retrieve someone who will be more than happy to lead you through the Papikonda Hills," Fullerton said as he straightened out his shirt.

Wilhelm crammed the bills into Fullerton's hand before he turned and disappeared down the road.

"You should've let me kill him," Ludwig said. "I could've made it look like he was mauled by a wild animal."

"No," Wilhelm said, shaking his index finger. "The British magistrate is right. We might have need of him yet. And he's going to join us for the journey."

CHAPTER 3

Calcutta, India

THE *GOLD SHELL* FINALLY REACHED PORT THREE DAYS later, safely delivering Richard to Calcutta. He completed all the paperwork required to receive his payment for working on the ship and collected his paltry earnings. On the shore, Slim awaited Richard while jangling a handful of coins.

"You ready to see the madness of India and burn through everything you just made?" Slim asked with a sly smile.

"That really depends on what you want to do," Richard said.

"I just want to show you a good time."

"I'm not sure that what constitutes a *good time* for you is the same for me."

"You only live once," Slim said. "Besides, with me as your tour guide, you can enter the city confidently knowing that you won't waste your time visiting places that won't provide you with the most value for your money."

Richard sighed. "I don't know, Slim. It's just that—"

He stopped midsentence as he saw an Indian man next to a rickshaw along the road with a shabby sign.

"What is it, Richard?" Slim asked as he turned to see what Richard was staring at.

Richard cocked his head to the side as he walked toward the man. "Who sent you?"

"Are you Mr. Halliburton?" the man asked.

Richard nodded. "You didn't answer my question though. Who sent you?"

"Dr. Knapp, of course. He said you might be resistant at first."

Richard exhaled slowly and put his hands on his hips. "Resistant? I don't even know who Dr. Knapp is, much less what he wants with me. As exciting as a ride in your rickshaw there looks, I'm afraid you're going to have to tell me more than that before I take one more step. And I'll warn you that even then it might not be enough to convince me."

"If you don't come with me, Mr. Halliburton, your life might be in danger."

Richard chuckled. "My life is always in danger, whether at the hands of someone else or by my own choosing. If you're not grappling with your own mortality, you're merely existing instead of truly living."

"But if you're dead by morning, no one will care about how you grappled with your mortality. You'll simply cease to exist. Now, you don't have much time as I'm sure the Reichswehr already know that their assassination plot against you failed."

Richard exhaled. "You do make an excellent point."

"So you'll come with me?"

"Do I really have a choice?"

"Not if you desire to live to see another sunrise."

Richard turned toward Slim. "Godspeed, my friend. Enjoy all that Calcutta has to offer. Perhaps we'll see each other again at sea."

Slim's mouth fell agape. "You—you're going with him?"

"Apparently, it's the only sensible thing to do," Richard

said, patting Slim on his shoulder.

"But I thought—"

"Good luck, Slim," Richard said as he strode toward the rickshaw. He climbed into the seat and looked back at his friend, who gave a halfhearted wave.

"We haven't been properly introduced," Halliburton said, offering his hand. "Richard Halliburton from Memphis, Tennessee."

"Anup Rahut from right here in Calcutta," the man answered as he shook Richard's hand.

Anup positioned himself to pull the cart and broke into a slow jog.

"So, who really sent you, Anup?" Richard asked.

Anup shot a quick glance over his shoulder at Richard. "Do you know a man named Hank Foster?"

"Perhaps," Richard said. "Was he the one who paid you to pick me up?"

Anup nodded. "I met him several years ago while waiting for a new client near the port. Mr. Foster always pays me well."

"He was here? In Calcutta?" Richard asked as his eyes widened.

"Several days ago he found me and asked me to look for the *Gold Shell* to dock. He said you'd be on it."

"And you're taking me to a Dr. Knapp?"

Anup shook his head and laughed. "No, I'm not taking you, but I've arranged for a train ticket for you."

"What's so funny?"

"Dr. Knapp lives in Dhamtari. It's about five hundred miles from here. You wouldn't catch me in that village in a million years. However, you might enjoy yourself there."

Richard furrowed his brow. "Why would you never go there but think I would enjoy it?"

"It's in the heart of the jungle, Mr. Halliburton. With wild animals prowling all around the village, you'll have plenty of opportunities to grapple with your mortality."

What are you up to this time, Hank?

* * *

THE RIDE ALONG THE RICKETY RAILS MADE RICHARD YEAR for a yawing sea, despite the fact that he'd secured a first class ticket. Anup had given Richard a third class rail pass, but he slipped the conductor some extra money to earn an upgrade at a far better bargain than purchasing one outright. Nevertheless, Richard wondered if he would ever reach Dhamtari after chugging along a route that appeared to be an endless jungle with brief respites of rural farming communities.

Several hours into the trip, the man sitting across from Richard finally spoke. "First time in India?"

Richard glanced at the man. He wore a monocle and had appeared engrossed by the contents of his edition of the Calcutta newspaper until now.

"Is it that obvious?" Richard replied.

The man smiled. "Well, you only need to take a train through India once to realize that staring out the window is a terrible way to pass the boredom. The only thing you'll see while on seemingly endless trips through the jungle is green vegetation with an occasional peak in the distance. You might as well be looking at the same picture for sixteen hours."

"I take it this is something you do quite often," Richard said.

"It's an unfortunate requirement of the job as a magistrate here. It's been three years since the Government of India Act passed, and we're still sorting out the mess."

"If it gives you any encouragement, aside from the heat and the foreign dress, I almost would've thought I was in England after we reached port in Calcutta."

"Then you didn't venture far enough into the city. The port is about the only thing that would be up to our standards. Everything else feels chaotic, which is how the people here prefer it. And as long as they're happy, parliament is satisfied."

The man began reading his newspaper again while Richard returned his gaze to the unchanging landscape, hoping to prove the man wrong with the sighting of some exotic wild animal. After a few more minutes, the man exchanged his paper for some documents he'd retrieved from his briefcase. Richard couldn't make out any of the contents, but he noticed the phrase "Top Secret" stamped on the outside.

After a half hour, the man returned the folder to his case and carried it with him as he left his seat. When he came back ten minutes later, he situated his belongings and then settled into his seat and closed his eyes. Five minutes later, he was asleep.

Richard waited for a few minutes before he sprang into action. He crept onto the floor next to the briefcase and jimmied open the lock. As he opened the top of the case, he found several dossiers. But only one of them was marked "Top Secret." Richard found it and opened the first page, the title jumping out at him: "Ancient Treasure: A Strategy for How to Tap India's Vast Hidden Resources."

Before he could read another word, the man moved, repositioning his feet and hitting Richard in the process. He rushed to slide the folder into the briefcase and latched it shut.

Richard's heart pounded in his chest, and he said a little prayer that the man seated across the aisle would remain asleep. In an effort to avoid suspicion, Richard closed his eyes and drifted off.

CHAPTER 4

Dhamtari, India

RICHARD AWOKE THE NEXT MORNING WHEN HE received a sharp jab from the conductor. "We're approaching your stop," he said.

Richard rubbed his eyes and glanced around the cabin. Several passengers remained aboard, but the British magistrate was gone.

"Are we in Dhamtari?" Richard asked.

"We will be in five minutes," the conductor said. "I thought you might want some extra time to gather all your belongings."

Richard thanked the man and collected his suitcase as well as his satchel and prepared to meet Dr. Knapp. Anup had given Richard a dossier that contained scant information about Dr. Knapp, most of it benign yet vital to identifying him. Richard couldn't help but wonder why he was assigned to visit a Mennonite mission in the middle of India.

After glancing at the picture of Dr. Knapp, Richard reread the protocol for greeting the man at the train depot. Once Richard assured himself that he understood who he was looking for, he identified Dr. Knapp. The missionary was seated on a bench and wearing a white linen shirt with the sleeves rolled up just past his elbow. He scanned each passenger as they stepped onto the platform.

Richard locked gazes with Dr. Knapp and strode up to him. "It's another fine day in India."

"Depends on what you fancy," Dr. Knapp said, his voice deep and gruff.

"Lions, tigers, and bears."

Dr. Knapp nodded. "We've got plenty of tigers, and I'll show them to you, if you're interested."

The exchange was all scripted according to the dossier's instructions, confirming for both men that they were meeting the right person.

"Let's take a walk," Dr. Knapp said as he stood.

Dr. Knapp remained quiet as he lumbered along the dusty road toward his compound. They walked for ten minutes through the burgeoning village's center. A marketplace situated in the middle appeared to serve as the heartbeat of the community. Everything from butter and eggs to blankets and clothes to iron-forged tools and wooden wheels were traded there. One woman approached Richard in an attempt to lure him to her booth, but Dr. Knapp gave her a stern look that promptly ended her hasty pitch.

They finally arrived at the mission, which was a walled compound located on the outskirts of town. Dr. Knapp nodded at the guard outside, who hustled to unlock the large gate and open it.

As they entered, Richard noticed a flurry of activity around the main courtyard. Several women huddled outside in rocking chairs while knitting clothing. A couple of men tended a small herd of goats in one corner, while a half dozen children worked with a supervisor to cultivate a small patch of dirt. It didn't take long for Richard to see why the locals treated Dr. Knapp with reverence. Introducing innovations from the west was slowly pushing the village into the 20th Century, and the people appeared eager to learn. Yet there was still a way about Dr. Knapp that made Richard think there was more to the missionary than what he revealed.

Dr. Knapp led Richard down a breezeway before taking a hard right down a dark corridor with a single door at the far end.

"Where are we going?" he asked.

Dr. Knapp stopped and eyed Richard carefully. "You're still wondering why you're here, aren't you?"

"I'd be lying if I denied it."

"Well, I'm about to show you," Dr. Knapp said before inserting a key into the lock and then putting his shoulder into the door. It creaked open and Richard followed Dr. Knapp into a dark room. He shuffled from one oil lamp to the next, lighting each one until the room was aglow.

In an instant, Richard realized that Dr. Knapp wasn't who he seemed. At the far end of the room were wooden cutouts of people, most of them riddled with holes. Against the wall were sandbags stacked floor to ceiling, designed to catch the bullets and soundproof the room. To Richard's right stood a large cache of weapons in an open chest.

"A Mennonite missionary," Richard said with a chuckle. "Are you now going to tell me what I'm really doing here?"

"Isn't it obvious?" Dr. Knapp said, making a sweeping gesture around the room with his hand. "I'm here to train you."

"To do what?"

"To fight and shoot better. I heard you had some close calls on your last assignment in Egypt, closer than they should've been according to Hank Foster."

"My *last* assignment?" Richard asked as he started to chuckle. "That was the *only* assignment I've ever had. Hank had just recruited me and threw me into the fray."

Dr. Knapp grinned. "That's the only way to do it. Do you think I knew anything about how to be a missionary before Army Intelligence assigned me to the middle of the jungle?"

"Based on what I saw earlier, you look like you figured it out."

"Yes, but I didn't have to learn it while my life was constantly being threatened. The only thing that posed real danger to me was something I already knew how to take care of—and something I'm going to show you how to handle later. But first things first. Show me what you've got in the realm of hand-to-hand combat."

Richard cocked his head to one side. "Really? I just—"

A swift jab to his midsection cut his response short. Dr. Knapp was already dancing around, bouncing on the balls of his feet as he darted from side to side. He went for an uppercut, but Richard was ready, narrowly avoiding a direct blow to his jaw and spinning into a leg kick that walloped Dr. Knapp in his side.

"Good," Dr. Knapp said as he staggered backward. "This is what I wanted to see. If I'm going to train you, I need to know what I'm working with before we begin."

Richard decided to show off the rest of his repertoire. Unleashing a flurry of punches at Dr. Knapp, Richard thought he was to teach his tutor a few things. But in the end, Richard's flashy moves were little more than sound and fury, summarily dismissed when he struggled to land a direct hit on the skilled Dr. Knapp. He only had to absorb one punch during the onslaught before putting Richard on his back in two swift moves.

"Thank you," Dr. Knapp said as he put his knee into Richard's chest and loomed over him. "Now I know I've got my work cut out for me."

* * *

FOR SIX DAYS, RICHARD TRAINED TWELVE HOURS A DAY, breaking only to eat and for short rests. Most of his mornings and afternoons were comprised of learning how to fight, but two hours were set aside for target practice at the secret indoor range. When the seventh day dawned, Richard was so sore that he wasn't convinced he could get out of bed when Dr. Knapp rapped on the door.

"Mr. Halliburton, it's time to get up," he said from the hallway.

"Even God rested one day during a week," Richard said with a slight moan.

"We're not training today—at least not hand-to-hand."

Richard rolled out of bed and then shuffled across the floor. He opened the door and peered into the hallway.

"You ready?" Dr. Knapp asked.

"What are we doing?"

"Get dressed, and I'll tell you on the way."

Richard hustled into his clothes and then exited his room, meeting Dr. Knapp in the breezeway just outside.

"Would you mind telling me what we're doing today?" Richard asked again.

"You're going to learn how to be a sniper."

"I'm going to shoot someone?" Richard asked, his eyes widening. "Today?"

"Not exactly."

Richard followed Dr. Knapp through a back gate. In less than a hundred meters, they had ventured into the thick jungle vegetation. Dr. Knapp slashed a path with his machete as the two men traveled along. After a half hour, Dr. Knapp stopped beside a stream and scanned the area.

"We'll go there," he said, gesturing up toward a tree with his blade.

"Are you finally going to tell me what we're doing out here?" Richard asked.

"We're going to catch a predator, one that's been terrorizing this village for a few weeks now."

"What kind of predator are we talking about? A wild animal?"

Dr. Knapp nodded. "Precisely. But more specifically, a tiger."

"I knew it," Richard said. "That guy on the train acted like I wouldn't see any wildlife like that here, but I just knew he was blowing me off for some reason."

"Was he British?"

"How did you know?"

Dr. Knapp laughed. "The British ruling class generally avoid the heart of India and never see the things everyone writes about and wants to see when they visit. They're almost in denial about what stalks around the villages and cities."

"And you obviously know better."

"Of course I do. I've lived here a long time. And let me assure you that if you can handle a tiger, you can handle any assignment U.S. Army Intelligence gives you. And if you don't . . ."

Richard didn't need Dr. Knapp to finish his statement. The implications were perfectly clear: Hunting a tiger was the most difficult assignment Richard could have, and if he couldn't pass it, he wouldn't make a very good agent. Richard also considered how he might also die if he didn't succeed.

"Is this how you sift through the pool of candidates?" Richard asked. "Or is it how you thin the predators around your village?"

Dr. Knapp shrugged. "A little of both, I guess. But it's been a while since we've had a fatality among any of our potential agents."

"I'm not sure I'm cut out for this."

"Sure you are. You love adventure and the danger that comes with it. This is the perfect job for you. What's more exciting than walking into a kill-or-be-killed situation?"

"I can think of plenty."

"But can any of those be helping your country while keeping other tyrants at bay?"

Richard didn't answer. Though he didn't want to, he had killed a man in Egypt. The thought of taking another human life wasn't appealing. However, in the scenario that Dr. Knapp was describing, Richard preferred to acquire the skills necessary to remain alive if ever forced into such a predicament.

They reached a small clearing, and then Dr. Knapp strode over to the base of a tree. Seemingly effortless, he ascended about three-quarters of the way to the top. Once situated on a thick branch, he beckoned Richard. While Dr. Knapp was the appointed expert, Richard scaled the tree more quickly than his guide.

"So, now what?" Richard asked as he settled onto a branch just below Dr. Knapp.

"Now we wait."

"You expect a tiger to just saunter by?"

"Only because I know my enemy," Dr. Knapp said. "You're learning how to be an assassin already, and you hardly even know it."

"Climbing a tree is an essential skill?"

"We found a favorable position and claimed it," Dr. Knapp said. "We also moved high enough to escape any potential immediate danger."

"But why this spot?"

"Detailed intelligence will dictate where the best potential locations are to target your enemy. For example, I've lived here long enough and observed the habits of this tiger to know he will walk by this area very soon."

"And we're just going kill this animal?" Richard asked with a scowl.

"He ate two small children last week who wandered off into the jungle."

"Maybe parents should be more watchful and we wouldn't have to shoot a gorgeous animal."

"There's nothing beautiful about watching a wild animal feast on human flesh, trust me."

They sat in silence for the next five minutes. Richard mulled over all that he'd heard, wondering if he'd have the guts to pull the trigger. Then he received his chance sooner than he'd imagined.

"There she is," Dr. Knapp whispered as he peered through his binoculars.

Richard scanned the opening and saw the large creature easing along the jungle floor without even the slightest of sounds. The moment was a peaceful one, captivating Richard's imagination. But it was cut short by a shrill yelp from Dr. Knapp.

"What is it?" Richard asked.

"A pit viper," Dr. Knapp said.

Richard looked up and saw a snake wrapped around a branch over head. The reptile hissed at Dr. Knapp>as he wielded his dagger. The predator drew back before striking. In an effort to fend off the viper, Dr. Knapp lost his balance and fell, hitting several branches before grabbing hold of one about ten meters off the ground.

"Are you all right?" Richard asked as he kept his eyes trained on the snake making his way around the branch overhead.

"I'll be fine as long as I can hold on," Dr. Knapp said.

Richard eased back toward the trunk, glancing down to see the tiger unfazed by the commotion as she looked up and circled Dr. Knapp's position.

"If I fall, she's going to devour me," Dr. Knapp said.

"And what do you expect me to do now?"

"Take the damn shot and kill this animal before it eats me for dinner."

Richard secured his rifle and scurried down a couple branches to put some distance between him and the viper. Then he assessed the situation below. With Dr. Knapp struggling to stay suspended, Richard needed to put the animal down—or at least scare it off.

"Remember what I taught you," Dr. Knapp said, his voice quivering. "Deep breath, squeeze the trigger."

"I got this," Richard said.

He placed the butt of the rifle against his shoulder and steadied his weapon on an adjacent branch. After taking aim, Richard followed Dr. Knapp's training. As Richard's finger eased the trigger back, the crack of the gun almost took him by surprise. He teetered on the limb before regaining his balance. Once he did, he looked down to see the results of his shot.

Instead of seeing a dead tiger, Richard realized that he had hit the animal enough to make it mad but not enough to kill it.

"Try again," Dr. Knapp said. "This time, your aim better be true."

The tiger's pace increased as she stared upward at Dr. Knapp. Without warning, Dr. Knapp's hand slipped and he tumbled another five meters before grabbing ahold of another branch.

"Richard, hurry it up, will you? I can't hold on much longer."

Dr. Knapp's feet dangled below without any nearby limb to gain solid footing, and the branch creaked and moaned as he attempted to still himself.

"Hold on," Richard said. "Just a few more seconds."

He chambered another round and was about to shoot when the viper hissed again. Richard abandoned his position, swinging over to another branch and then scurrying down another ten meters.

"It's been more than a few seconds," Dr. Knapp said.

"Almost there," Richard said before hastily preparing to take a shot.

After lining up the tiger with the bead through the sight, Richard took a deep breath and fired another shot. This time, the bullet flew true, striking the beast in the center of his chest.

Richard winced as he watched the animal claw her way along the ground before stopping a few meters beyond the clearing.

Dr. Knapp let go of the branch and fell to the jungle floor, collapsing in a heap. Richard hustled down the tree and rushed over to check on his mentor.

"Are you okay?" Richard asked.

Dr. Knapp nodded as he rubbed his right arm. "I'll live, thanks to you."

Richard crept over toward the tiger to inspect what he'd done, though he could barely stand to look at her.

Joining Richard, Dr. Knapp threw his arm around his pupil. "I know that was hard for you, but it had to be done. That same tiger ravaged two small children and would've gladly done the same to me given the opportunity."

"That still doesn't make it any easier," Richard said. "Just look at her. She's a magnificent beast."

"And sometimes great danger accompanies an animal like

this. Don't mistake beauty for safety. Such an assumption could end your life as an intelligence agent."

"But did we have to kill her?" Richard asked, gesturing toward the animal.

"Yes," Dr. Knapp said before pulling out his pistol and shooting the tiger in the head. "And the most humane thing we can do is end her suffering. Now, let's get back to the compound and tell everyone the good news."

Richard felt sick to his stomach over what he'd done as he trudged along. He wanted to experience the beauty of nature, not destroy it.

"You're awfully quiet back there," Dr. Knapp said. "Are you all right?"

Richard sighed. "I've been better."

"Look, the charge of taking another person's life is a grave matter, even if that person deserves it. But sometimes we must do things we find unsavory to protect the loss of even greater bloodshed, particularly to the innocent. That tiger was a perfect example. Now, I'm not going to tell you how to be an intelligence officer, because each person has to travel his own path. You do what works best for each situation—and you do it however you need to keep your conscience clear. Besides, the fact that you even have one is always a good sign. It'll guide your steps and keep you moored on the side of doing what's right when the best choice isn't always so obvious."

"I hope so," Richard said. "If I lose my conscience, every good thing I've ever done on this earth will be overshadowed by the fact that I couldn't maintain the bearing I needed to leave this world better than I found it."

"If you're even thinking about that now means that you have a good chance to navigate this position better than most."

Once they reached the compound, they entered through the back gate, slipping inside without anyone noticing their weapons. Dr. Knapp unlocked his training room and replaced all the guns.

"Come with me," Dr. Knapp said, gesturing for Richard to follow him.

Dr. Knapp strode to his main office and offered Richard a seat once they both got inside.

"What's this all about?" Richard asked.

Dr. Knapp sat down across from Richard and leaned forward. "I wanted to let you know that I'm recommending your approval to proceed as a U.S. Army intelligence officer. You're ready, Richard. And I don't think I'll ever see a finer man in my lifetime.

"Thank you, sir," Richard said. "I appreciate your kind and encouraging words."

"I can assure you that's not the norm. I rarely approve agents so quickly. However, I always get them a gift."

"A gift?"

Dr. Knapp nodded and reached inside his desk drawer, producing a small box. He placed it in front of Richard. "Go ahead. Open it."

Richard lifted the lid and then reached inside, taking hold of a silver belt buckle. He maintained a straight face, trying not to give away his sense of bewilderment.

"Looks like a normal buckle, doesn't it?" Dr. Knapp asked as he held his hand out. "But looks can be deceiving."

Richard handed the metal object back to Dr. Knapp, who pulled down on the latch to reveal a small knife. "You never know when you might need this to get out of a jam."

"Thank you," Richard said. "I'm sure this might come in handy one day."

"And on that note, I thought you might want to learn

about your first assignment after you've gotten some training."

Dr. Knapp pushed a sealed envelope toward Richard. He picked it up and opened it quickly. He scanned the page before re-reading it again very slowly.

Richard cocked his head to one side and scowled. "It says I'm going to have a partner for this trip and that he'll meet me on the train in the morning at the Dhamtari depot."

"What's the assignment?" Dr. Knapp asked.

Richard furrowed his brow as he glanced at the paper again. "It doesn't say."

CHAPTER 5

Wilhelm glanced at his watch, unsure if Alex Fullerton would ever return with a suitable guide. With the way the British magistrate was acting, Wilhelm wondered if Fullerton had simply absconded with the money. Despite the dire warning, the Reichswehr leader wasn't intimidated about what lurked in the Papikonda Hills. Guide or no guide, he was confident his elite team of soldiers could handle any attack by Thugs with primitive weapons.

"Do you want me to go after him?" Ludwig asked.

Wilhelm peered down the path and shook his head. "We'll give him five more minutes."

The rest of the Reichswehr troops were busy securing their supplies and gear for the next leg of their journey when Fullerton reappeared less than a minute later. He had a guide in tow who wore a wide grin on his face as he bounced along the trail.

"Everyone, this is Mahendra," Fullerton announced. "He was born in these hills and knows them better than anyone. In fact, he used to be a part of the Thugs that roam these forests, so he knows better than anyone how to avoid them."

Wilhelm eyed Fullerton closely. "I wasn't sure you were coming back."

"Whatever would give you that idea?" Fullerton asked.

"I don't know, but you're coming with us," Wilhelm said.

Fullerton's eyes widened. "I'm afraid that's not possible. I have work to attend to here, and I can't waste my time traipsing through the jungle with your team."

Ludwig stepped in front of Fullerton. "It wasn't a request."

Fullerton sighed and shook his head. "Am I your insurance policy? You want me to make sure that this man is going to do what you're paying him to do?"

"You talk too much," Wilhelm said as he shoved Fullerton down the path.

Fullerton stopped and looked back at the elephants. "What are you going to do about those animals? You can't just leave them here."

"Consider it a bonus for when you return," Wilhelm said. "I'm sure you'll find some way to make a profit off them."

Fullerton nodded. "Give me a minute."

With Ludwig following closely behind, Fullerton hustled over toward one of the villagers and had a brief conversation before returning.

"Ready?" Wilhelm asked.

Fullerton nodded.

"Then let's go," Wilhelm said.

Mahendra was in the middle of introducing himself to each soldier and shaking their hands before Wilhelm interrupted with a more stern order to begin the journey. Fullerton explained that once they navigated through the Papikonda Hills, the soldiers would find much less dangerous terrain as well as a train depot that would allow them to go wherever they wanted far more efficiently. Without any animals to assist in their trip, he warned that the journey could be lengthy.

"How long are you talking about?" Wilhelm asked.

"Several days at least," Fullerton answered.

"Tell Mahendra we need it completed in two."

"We'll never make it that quickly," Fullerton protested.

"My men are highlytrained soldiers. The terrain is of little concern to them. They care only about the end goal. And if that is to emerge from the jungle in two days, they'll do whatever it takes to do that. So, you better not slow us down."

Fullerton swallowed hard and nodded.

* * *

THE CARAVAN PICKED ITS WAY THROUGH THE VEGETATION behind Mahendra's guidance. After an hour, the group took its first water break near a stream. Wilhelm announced it would last no more than two minutes before settling onto a rock next to Fullerton, who was lying on the ground.

"Still think we won't be able to make it in two days?" Wilhelm asked.

"If your men can keep up this pace, perhaps it's possible, but I'm not the one to be asking," Fullerton said. "Mahendra is the man who knows these woods like the back of his hand."

"And how long have you known our guide?"

"Long enough to know he's one of the best in this region, not to mention that I trust him fully. He's proven to be a valuable asset in our fight to curtail all the thievery in the area."

"In that case, we're lucky to have him," Wilhlem said as he stood. "Let's get going. Break's over."

The Reichswehr soldiers scrambled to get up and resume their journey along the path. However, they hadn't been hiking for more than five minutes more before a young boy sprinted toward them. Hunched over with his hands on his knees, he tried to catch his breath. After a few seconds, he said something, though he struggled to get it out.

Mahendra and the young boy had an exchange in Hindi before the guide translated everything. Once the message was fully received, Mahendra looked up, wide-eyed.

"There are some Thugs around the next bend in the road," Mahendra explained. "We need to take another route. Follow me. I know a way around them."

All the soldiers glanced at Wilhelm, who wasn't interested in instigating a conflict, though he wasn't afraid of one either. He nodded, conveying assurance as he did.

"If that's what we have to do, then follow him," he said before glancing at Ludwig. When the pair made eye contact, Ludwig nodded.

Mahendra guided the group down a small hill near a stream. After walking parallel with it for a few minutes, they rounded a bend and came to a stop near the base of another hill. At first glance, there didn't appear to be a way out.

"What's this?" Wilhelm asked.

Before he could do anything, a dozen Thugs emerged from the surrounding trees. Most of the men were armed with swords and daggers, while the leader carried a pistol. The boy ran up to the leader.

"Good job, son," the leader said, tousling the boy's hair. He looked up and smiled at the man.

"What is this?" Wilhelm demanded.

"You're being robbed," Mahendra said with a faint smile.

Wilhelm turned toward Fullerton. "You set us up."

"I—I had no idea he was going to do this," Fullerton said.

The bandits' leader stepped forward, waving his gun toward the Reichswehr soldiers. "Place your weapons on the ground, and throw all your valuables over here."

"Why would I do such a thing?" Wilhelm asked.

The man shrugged. "Maybe you would prefer that I take everything off your dead bodies. It makes no difference to me. You decide."

Wilhelm glanced into the woods behind the thieves. "I suggest you put down your weapons and return to where you came from."

The man laughed. "Why would I do that?"

"Because you're surrounded," Wilhelm said.

At that moment, Ludwig and several other soldiers stepped out of the forest with their guns trained on the Thugs.

The leader glared at Mahendra. "You set us up."

Mahendra stared back, eyes wide and mouth agape. "I thought everyone was with me, and I—"

Swinging his gun in Mahendra's direction, the leader narrowed his eyes. "It was a simple task, yet you failed me again."

"Put the gun down now," Wilhelm said. "I need our guide."

The man laughed. "A guide? He can hardly find his way from one village to another. I don't know where you're expecting him to guide you to, but you should consider hiring someone else."

"Like who? You?"

The leader nodded. "I'm far more capable of taking you through the Papikonda Hills than this man."

"If you don't lower your weapon right now, you won't be leading anyone anywhere anymore," Wilhelm said. "Is that clear?"

The leader made a quick move toward Wilhelm before he gunned the man the down. Two of the other Thugs appeared to be wheeling their weapons in Wilhelm's direction but didn't get far as Ludwig and another Reichswehr soldier shot both men.

"I'm not going to ask again," Wilhelm said.

The rest of the bandits dropped their guns on the ground and raised their hands in the air. Ludwig directed his fellow agents as they tied the Thugs to nearby trees.

Mahendra glanced at Wilhelm. "Do you still need a guide?"

"Any more shenanigans and I won't hesitate to shoot you. Understood?"

Mahendra nodded. "Thank you, sir, for trusting me."

"I don't trust you, but I don't have any other options at this point. You better make yourself indispensable."

Wilhelm then turned his attention toward Fullerton.

"I'm terribly sorry about all this," Fullerton said. "If I would've thought that this man would—"

"I'm not interested in listening to your excuses," Wilhelm said. "The only thing keeping you alive right now is the fact that you might be able to help us if we ever get out of this godforsaken jungle. If it weren't for that fact, you'd be joining these Thugs here."

"I won't let you down."

"It's too late for that," Wilhelm said. "But there still might be a chance for you to redeem yourself."

"What do you want me to do?" Fullerton asked.

"I want you to return to your village along with one of my men and spread the word that the Thugs' actions will not be tolerated anymore, and that you intend to make an example out of them."

"But I can't do that. I'll—"

"You can and you will," Wilhelm said. "I'll send one of my men to accompany you to ensure that this happens."

Fullerton continued to protest, but Wilhelm ignored the pleas. A few minutes later, Ludwig reported that all the prisoners were secure.

"Time to move out," Wilhelm said. "We have a treasure to hunt."

CHAPTER 6

RICHARD THUMBED THROUGH A COPY OF *THE TIMES OF India* as he sat on the Dhamtari platform awaiting the train. When it finally arrived, he scanned the departing passengers, searching for someone who appeared to be looking for him. The quest proved fruitless when the conductor made the final call for boarding. Richard sighed as he stood, resigning himself to the fact that either something had gone wrong or he had misinterpreted the message.

He trudged onto the locomotive and found his seat in a carriage compartment that had only one other occupant, a man wearing a dark suit who appeared to be in his early thirties. Once the train lurched forward and started chugging down the tracks, he got up and locked the doors.

"Mr. Halliburton, I suspect we should get acquainted," the man said.

"You're my contact?" Richard asked. "I was told that you would meet me on the platform at Dhamtari. This isn't following protocol."

The man wagged his index finger. "One thing you'll quickly learn about me is that I'm not a fan of the rules. I consider them mere guidelines, especially where it concerns areas that demand a more creative type of action."

"I think we'll get along famously," Richard said.

"David Wilson," the man said, extending his hand. "U.S. Army Intelligence."

Richard shook it and asked to see some credentials. David obliged and held out a badge along with the corresponding passport.

"Hank Foster told me you'd be cautious and not to deviate from the plan," David said.

"Yet here you are."

"Well, it's not by some small chance either. There is a greater force in the universe that still wants me alive."

Richard furrowed his brow. "Did you survive a harrowing near-death experience?"

"*A* harrowing experience? As in only *one*?"

Richard nodded.

"More like dozens," David said, "but this latest one was the most danger I've ever been in. I was certain I was going to die, but I guess it's not my time."

"What happened?"

David winced. "I'm not really at liberty to say, but just know that my partner at the time didn't make it."

"I'm sorry to hear that."

"Don't be," David said. "He was a pompous blowhard, full of himself and stuck on living in the glory of his past accomplishments instead of working hard to secure the future. It was his own arrogance that led to his death—and *nearly* killed me."

"On that note, do you have any idea what this assignment entails?" Richard asked.

"We're going to receive further details at the next stop on our journey, but all I know for now is that it involves a secret Reichswehr unit that you are allegedly quite familiar with."

Richard nodded. "From what I've gathered, they're

hunting treasures all across the world as a way to build up their war chest outside the auspices of the Treaty of Versailles. And we must stop them."

"Sounds simple enough."

"Hardly," Richard said. "They're an elite group of men trained for battle and equipped to handle anything thrown in their direction. Whatever they're up to India, I can assure you that nothing about it will be simple."

"I heard you handled them on your own in Egypt. Couldn't be that hard, right?"

"Beginner's luck," Richard said. "They had their chance to kill me before—and I doubt they'll pass up an opportunity like that again. If they can, they will eliminate me."

David chuckled. "How does a travel writer get involved in espionage without any formal training?"

"Hank Foster offered me two things that I struggle to turn down: money and adventure. But to be honest, it was more about the money, though I'm slowly learning to enjoy the adventure. For example, I have no idea where we're going, and the thought of that is exhilarating."

"No wonder Foster pursued you," David said. "You sound far crazier than you look, though it's quite apparent just how insane you truly are."

"I'll take that as a compliment. However, I'm curious. Where are we going?"

"Ever heard of Simla?"

Richard shook his head as David stood and opened the door to their compartment. "Is it just me, or is it kind of stuffy in here?"

Richard loosened his tie. "I've been here long enough to know that I constantly feel hot and stuffy."

A man with a monkey in tow stopped near the entryway. Squawking and hand extended, the animal swaggered up to

Richard. He hunched down and looked the animal in the eye before making some clicking noises. The monkey reciprocated before turning and snatching David's hat off his head and giving it to Richard.

The monkey's owner laughed. "Well done."

"How did you do that?" David asked, his mouth agape.

"I learned a few tricks when I was in Gibraltar," Richard said. "Never know when you might need to entertain someone on the spot."

* * *

WHEN THE TRAIN ARRIVED IN SIMLA, A PORTER MET DAVID and Richard on the platform and helped hustle them to a carriage waiting outside. They posed as businessmen traveling to India to discuss a potential tea import opportunity to the United States.

After twenty minutes of bumping along the rough road, they arrived at the large estate of Mr. Harvey Carrington and were ushered inside along with all their baggage. A butler greeted them with a silver platter containing freshly brewed tea and pastries. He informed Richard and David that Mr. Carrington would be down momentarily and join them in the library.

While David took a seat on the couch, Richard stared at the floor-to-ceiling bookshelves, each spot filled. He sauntered over to the far wall and ran his fingers along the fine mahogany shelves, studying the titles to determine what kind of stories Mr. Carrington liked to read.

"Find something that suits your fancy?" a man asked.

Richard spun around to see a tall man sporting a gray suit with a vest adorned by a gold pocket watch. He used his thumb and forefinger to smooth out his mustache, which was sufficiently oiled and pressed flat against his face.

"I notice you're fond of Nathaniel Hawthorne," Richard said.

"Fond is not nearly a strong enough word to convey my true affections for the man's writing."

The man strode over toward Richard and offered his hand. "Harvey Carrington. And I presume you must be Richard Halliburton."

Richard nodded. "Yes, sir, though I'm not sure if I should be concerned or impressed that you know who I am."

"Neither," Harvey said with a wink. "I've met with David before. You were the only new acquaintance scheduled to darken my door today."

"Well, I'm anxious to hear about what we're doing here," Richard said.

Harvey gestured toward the couch. "Please, have a seat. We have plenty to discuss."

Richard eased onto the vacant half of the couch next to David and leaned forward. "What are the Germans up to now?"

"As you know so well, the Germans are on a hunt to uncover every major treasure they can get their hands on in this part of the world. The most difficult part is tracking them, though we have several agents who've been able to intercept messages and figure out where the Reichswehr unit is headed. This time, the only information we were able to obtain was the country."

David sighed and shook his head. "India is a vast place. Finding Wilhelm is going to be like looking for a needle in a haystack."

"I once helped find a dime in a haystack for my little brother when the coin fell out of his pocket while playing King of the Mountain," Richard said.

"Then maybe Foster knows what he's doing pairing us together," David said. "But I'm thinking this will actually be far more difficult."

Harvey picked up his teacup sitting on the silver tray and poured in a splash of milk before taking a sip.

"Do we know anything yet?" Richard asked.

"The Reichswehr troop has been seen in southern India, though we have reason to believe it's not their final destination," Harvey said. "According to our intelligence, the Reichswehr has indicated that their primary objective is to amass a fortune, one large enough to get them back on the world stage as a military power. And with the Treaty of Versailles being what it is, it's going to be a challenge to build up a cache of wealth. And extrapolating out what we know, it's likely they aren't going to waste their time hunting treasures in the south. All the substantial jewels and gold are in the central and northern section of the country."

"That doesn't exactly narrow it down," David said.

"And that's why you need to follow them," Harvey said. "On this assignment, the two of you will tail the Germans until you can determine where they're going and what they're doing. Once you do, you'll contact us and we'll send in an elite group of U.S. Army soldiers to secure the Reichswehr and hopefully learn more about what their country is doing, particularly Karl Wilhelm."

"Where are they now?" Richard asked.

"They were last seen in the Papikonda Hills," Harvey said. "But that was several days ago. Until we hear more, you need to sit and wait—and be ready to pursue them on a moment's notice."

CHAPTER 7

THE NEXT MORNING, RICHARD AND DAVID WERE finishing breakfast when a loud rapping on the front door startled both men. Harvey, who was sipping his tea and reading the paper, folded it up and slammed it on the table. He stood and huffed.

"People here just don't understand that you don't need to beat the door down in order to get someone to answer it," Harvey said before stomping to his office just off the entryway.

Richard followed Harvey, stopping short as a young Indian boy talked excitedly.

"Slow down, Adi," Harvey said. "I can barely understand what you're saying."

"I have a telegram, and it's urgent," Adi said, slowing down as he handed a piece of paper to Harvey.

Harvey scanned the note and then tousled Adi's hair. "Excellent work. Here's a little extra for your troubles."

Harvey depressed a silver coin into Adi's hand. He looked up and smiled before darting out the door and down the steps.

"Good news?" Richard asked as David joined him in the hallway.

"Gentlemen, you don't have a second to lose," Harvey said. "You need to pack your bags. One of our sources reported that the German contingent was in a port city on the east coast, asking about a certain British magistrate in Maredumilli."

"And where is that?" David asked.

"In the middle of the jungle."

"What would Reichswehr be doing there?" Richard asked.

Harvey grinned. "That's what you're going to find out."

* * *

WHEN THE TWO MEN ARRIVED IN MAREDUMILLI TWO DAYS later, Richard was even more bewildered than before as to the purpose of the Germans' visit to the village. With little commerce to speak of, there seemed to be no obvious reason to go so far out of the way. But Richard had learned by now that the Reichswehr unit worked to mask its intentions.

David insisted the trip be short since he speculated that the Germans wouldn't still be there.

"Maybe there's more to this village than we know," Richard said.

David shook his head. "If there's a rumor about a treasure in this part of India, I would've heard about it by now. Those stories are shared freely and often. It's an Indian pastime. And everyone knows the legends about where the supposed troves of jewels and gold are hidden. As someone who is well-versed in these tales, I can assure you this small village isn't on the list."

"Perhaps the British magistrate will tell us why the Germans came here."

David huffed a soft laugh through his nose. "We have no authority to compel him to tell us anything. I doubt he'll talk."

"Sometimes people say plenty without saying a word."

"Well, I'll await your translation then when we see this official."

Richard and David asked around before they found a man who spoke English and agreed to take them to the magistrate's office. After they were on the steps to the building, David flipped the man a coin and trudged upward as Richard knocked on the door.

Moments later, a woman opened it and ushered them inside.

"We were hoping to speak to the magistrate," David said.

The brunette eyed him carefully. "And you're assuming that I'm not the magistrate because I'm a woman."

David blushed. "No, it's just that—"

She laughed and waved dismissively. "I'm just giving you some grief. I'll let the magistrate know you're here."

She strode across the room and knocked on a door. A man wearing a gray suit answered and stepped into the hallway at the woman's request. He furrowed his brow as he walked across the room, intently studying his two visitors.

"Is there something I can help you gentlemen with?" he asked.

"Indeed there is, Mr. . . ." Richard said.

"Fullerton. Alex Fullerton," the man said as he studied his two guests.

"We're searching for a group of about a dozen Germans," David said. "They're members of the Reichswehr and rumored to be conducting operations which fall outside the guidelines of the Treaty of Versailles. You wouldn't have happened to have seen these gentlemen?"

Fullerton sighed and looked skyward. "We don't get many visitors here, so I'm sure I would've seen or heard about them if they were here, but I don't recall seeing any group of people that would fit that description."

"Perhaps they presented themselves as something other than soldiers," Richard suggested. "Or maybe they didn't even consider themselves German. Have you had any large group come through here in the past week or so?"

Fullerton shook his head. "I'm not sure we've ever had a group that large come through here since I've held this position—unless it was a family visiting relatives or for a funeral."

"In that case, do you mind if we inquire with others?" David asked.

"Be my guest," Fullerton said. "You can leave your bags here and I'll be happy to introduce you to some of the village's more influential people who would know if a group like that came through."

Richard and David stacked their bags on a chair in Fullerton's office and then followed him outside. Villagers smiled and waved at the trio as they walked along the dusty roads. While the area wasn't well developed, Richard noticed the British influence right away with a postal station and the thatched roofs atop newer structures.

"I know this place may seem primitive to you," Fullerton said as he strolled along, "but I can assure you that there's more than meets the eye with these people. They're extremely diligent workers and seem hungry to join the 20th Century and all she has to offer."

After they walked along for a couple minutes, Fullerton called out to a gentleman standing outside a blacksmith shop.

"Kabir," Fullerton said, "I have some people here who have a question for you."

Kabir wiped his hands with a rag before dabbing his forehead, which was covered in a mixture of sweat and black soot. He smiled and nodded at Richard and David.

"We were wondering if you've seen a group of about a

dozen Germans come through here recently?" David asked. "They would've been difficult to miss."

Kabir cut his eyes over at Fullerton before refocusing on David. "You're right. I would have noticed a large number of people like that, but I don't remember seeing them. And even if I didn't see it, people would've been talking about it. As you can tell, that would be quite the topic of conversation here."

Richard forced a smile and nodded, watching intently as Kabir glanced back at Fullerton.

"Thank you, Kabir," Fullerton said. "We don't want to take up any more of your time."

Fullerton repeated the process three more times with other villagers he deemed as prominent and influential. All of them seemed to look to Fullerton for a signal on how to answer. And all of them denied seeing the Germans.

"I'm afraid this is going to be an exercise in futility," Fullerton said. "This community is small, and it's not likely that a team of Germans could move through this town without attracting at least some attention. If no one we've spoken with by now saw them, I can all but guarantee you that they weren't here."

"Well, that is truly bewildering," David said. "We have reliable sources who say they were here."

"Is it possible that your source made a mistake?" Fullerton asked.

"Anything's possible, I guess," David said, "including a group of German soldiers slipping into your village right beneath your nose."

Fullerton stroked his chin. "I think we know which of those two scenarios is more likely. Now, if you'll please excuse me, I have a lot of work to get to."

David and Richard collected their bags and headed out

the door. Once they reached the bottom of the steps, Fullerton called to them.

"Just what do you think you're doing?" he asked.

Richard spun around to see Fullerton hustling toward them.

"I'm sorry," Richard said. "Are you talking to us?"

"Does it look like I'm speaking to anyone else?" Fullerton asked. "I knew something wasn't right about you two."

"What on Earth are you going on about?" David asked.

Fullerton whistled and waved for a constable to come over. The officer darted across the street and asked Fullerton what was going on.

"I think these men stole a valuable article out of my office," Fullerton said. "Please search their bags."

"This is ridiculous," David said as he opened his pack for the officer to peer into.

After finding nothing, he turned toward Richard. "Let me see your bag, sir."

Richard shrugged and handed over his sack. "I hate to disappoint you, but you're not going to find anything in there."

"Is that so?" the constable said.

"Yes, sir."

"Then what's this?" the officer asked as he pulled out a small golden idol.

"You thief," Fullerton shouted. "I paid more than fifty pounds for that item. And you just swiped it off my shelves. I should've trusted my instincts about the two of you."

"What should I do with them? Escort them out of the city?" the constable asked.

"No, let's make an example out of them," Fullerton said. "This type of mischief shouldn't be tolerated in any Indian village, no matter how small. Put them in the prison."

Richard's eyes widened. "I did not put that in my bag, and you know it. Be a reasonable man. I was with you every second since I stepped foot inside the magistrate building."

"Save your complaints for the court," Fullerton said.

"And you'll be the one presiding over the proceedings?" David asked.

Fullerton nodded. "That's what I do here." He turned toward the officer. "Take them away."

Richard didn't resist, even though for a moment he considered breaking into a sprint and seeing if anyone could catch him. The constable guided David and Richard toward a small structure across the street with a sign hanging over the doorway that read: "Maredumilli Police Station."

Richard glanced over his shoulder toward the magistrate standing on the steps of his building and smiling with his arms crossed. Behind him, a man peeked around the corner and appeared to be looking right at the two arrestees.

But it wasn't just any man. Richard knew that face from somewhere, but he couldn't quite place it. After a few more seconds of pondering who it was, he remembered.

"We were set up," Richard whispered. "And I know who did it."

"Please tell me who, Sherlock," David said.

"The Reichswehr did it—and they're still here."

CHAPTER 8

ALEX FULLERTON CLOSED THE DOOR TO HIS OFFICE the door to his office and sat down behind his desk. He lit another candle and prepared to start writing when he glanced up to see someone standing in the corner of the room. Surprised by the presence of another person, Fullerton knocked over his inkwell.

"What are you doing in here?" Fullerton asked. "You're supposed to stay out of sight."

"We have a serious problem," Felix Ludwig said. "And I need to take care of it promptly."

"This isn't Germany. You can't just kill your enemies here and get away with it. There's still some modicum of civility remaining in the British empire."

"Don't worry. I'll protect you. Nothing will happen on your watch."

Fullerton closed his eyes and rubbed his face. "This was a mistake."

"No, it wasn't," Ludwig said. "The mistake would've been resisting my request. I told you that I'd make sure they were able to be arrested for a crime. And now comes the easy part: Release them, and let me take care of the rest."

"Release them? Right now? We haven't even had a hearing, and one isn't scheduled until late tomorrow morning."

"This needs to be taken care of as soon as possible. That man in your prison—Richard Halliburton—he's responsible for the deaths of several fellow soldiers, and there has been no accountability for him."

Fullerton scowled as he scrubbed his desk clean. "He doesn't look like a hardened criminal to me. Are you sure?"

"Wilhelm wouldn't have insisted on keeping you alive if it weren't for the possibility that you could help us further by protecting us. This is the kind of protection he's referring to."

"I thought Wilhelm wanted me to ensure your safe passage across the country so you could travel without fear of being apprehended," Fullerton said. "This seems like something entirely different."

"Mr. Halliburton was supposed to be dead, but he must've escaped somehow. And you have the power to let me correct a mistake and serve justice to him."

Fullerton sighed but said nothing.

"I'll also contribute another hundred pounds to your fee," Ludwig said.

Fullerton finished wiping up the last inkblot on his desk and dropped the rag into the waste bin. "That's quite a large amount."

"It's a small price to pay considering how desperately we are to rid the earth of this vile murderer."

"All right, I'll do it on the condition that you don't kill him anywhere near this village. I don't want any more authorities swarming around and asking probing questions. Agreed?"

Ludwig nodded. "I can abide by that."

"Good," Fullerton said. "I'll release them both on a technicality, and they should be out of the village after lunchtime. Then you can track them down and handle your quarrel with Mr. Halliburton and his companion however you see fit."

Fullerton heard a loud creak out in the main section of the office. He dashed across the room and opened the door. There was nobody in sight, and the front door was bolted shut.

"What is it?" Ludwig asked.

"I thought I heard someone," Fullerton said.

"Is your assistant here?"

"No, she went home a long time ago."

"You're just being paranoid then. But don't worry. I'll make sure nobody can connect the disappearance of Mr. Halliburton and his colleague to you or this area. Now, go home and get some rest."

Fullerton opened the window and gestured toward it. "You go first. I'm not leaving you alone in here."

He watched Ludwig climb through the opening and disappear into the darkness. Fullerton then poured himself a glass of brandy before counting the money in the envelope Wilhelm had given him. While serving in India had been an interesting experience, Fullerton longed to return to London. And another hundred pounds combined with all the other money he'd saved up, he figured it would be enough to start a new life back home like he'd always dreamed of.

Just one more thing to do.

CHAPTER 9

RICHARD SETTLED ONTO ONE OF THE TWO COTS IN THE room and buried his head in his hands. He glanced at his partner, who wasn't handling their imprisonment well. With clenched fists, he banged on the frame of the bed and cursed under his breath.

"We'll get out of this," Richard said.

David sighed. "And how exactly are we going to do that? It'll take days before we can get word to Harvey about what this crooked judge is trying to do to us. And even then, there's no guarantee we'll be set free."

"I've been in worse situations," Richard said. "There's nothing wrong with a healthy dose of optimism."

"I wish I could share in that with you."

Richard glanced on the far wall and looked at the clock. "You can. It's only five-thirty. There's still time for the magistrate to correct his mistaken judgment of us."

"Maybe I'd feel better if I wasn't so hungry," David said.

A few minutes later, the constable shuffled inside the room, carrying a pair of food trays, and unlocked the prison gate. Then he retrieved the meals and placed them on the ground before relocking the cell. After hanging up the keys on a rack on the far side of the room, he exited without another word.

"He was afraid to look us in the eye," Richard said.

"The coward knows we're innocent," David said. "He was just doing the magistrate's bidding."

The two men devoured the food and then slid the trays through the bars. Richard wanted room to do pushups and challenged David to a competition.

"You really want to do this?" David asked.

"Anything to keep your mind off our situation," Richard said with a grin.

Just as the pair dropped to the floor, Richard scrambled to his knees at the high-pitched sound that squawked loudly.

"Do you hear that?" Richard asked.

"Sounds like a monkey," David said.

"That's exactly what I was thinking."

Richard strained to look around the corner of the wall, doing his best to peer into the small opening to the left of their cell where the noise seemed to emanate from. He looked up at the barred windows near the ceiling above the entrance but still didn't see anything.

"I know it's in here," Richard said.

David jumped to his feet and rushed over to the bars. He grabbed them and furrowed his brow as he looked into a portion of the office.

"There he is," David said, pointing beneath the desk. "Do that thing you do where you call the monkey and tell them what to do."

"This isn't the same type of situation,"

"I don't care," David said. "Just try it. What do we have to lose?"

Richard shrugged and took a deep breath before emitting a high-pitched frequency and then making a clicking sound. The monkey peeked around the edge of the desk and stared at Richard.

"Come over here, little buddy," he said. "I'm not gonna hurt you. I want you to help us. And maybe we can help you."

The monkey flashed his teeth before turning his back on Richard.

"Oh, for goodness sake, we have a temperamental monkey," David said. "Of all the monkeys in the world, we get the one that—"

"Almost all monkeys are like this," Richard said, cutting short David's rant. "You have to be patient."

Richard grabbed a few pieces of the biscuit leftover on his tray and held them out for the monkey. The furry creature bounded over and snatched the morsels out of his hand. Without hesitating or a thorough inspection, the animal crammed the food into his mouth. He screeched with delight.

"What are you doing?" David said. "You just gave him all the motivation we had—and for what? Now we can't coax him to do anything for us."

Richard looked up and wagged his index finger at David. "That's where you're wrong. Once you make a monkey your friend, he stays your friend. Just watch."

Returning his focus to the animal, Richard gestured with his hands for the creature to retrieve the keys on the wall. The monkey scampered onto the chair beneath the desk and stretched to reach the keys. Once he wrapped his hand around them, he yanked them back and teetered before quickly regaining his balance.

"That's it," Richard said, waving the animal toward him. "Just bring the keys to papa."

The animal was about halfway across the room before the door swung open and several constables entered. He glanced at Richard, who was still crouched down with both hands extended through the bars. Then the officer made eye contact with the monkey, who squealed and dropped the keys.

He scurried outside despite the constable's demands.

"Riki, you get back here at once," he said. "You know better than to do that."

He knelt down and collected the keys before storming toward the prisoners. In a fit of fury, he unlocked the door and chained David to the wall. Once the constable was finished, he flicked his whip.

"What are you doing?" Richard asked as he scrambled to get away.

"Something I should've done before I threw you troublemakers in here."

Before the beating continued, the magistrate appeared in the doorway. "Reginald, what are you doing? You know that's no way to treat our guests."

The constable stopped and looked sheepishly over his shoulder at Fullerton.

"Here to admit you were wrong about us?" Richard asked.

Reginald unchained David before leaving the cell and locking it back.

"If you think I'm about to release you, you're quite mistaken," Fullerton said. "I simply stopped by to let you know that your barrister will be by to visit with you in the morning."

"You should recuse yourself from this case," David said with a sneer. "It's the only right thing to do."

"If I could, I would gladly do so. However, there's not another magistrate who could get here within three days, and I think it's more just to expedite your hearing than it is to get someone else to hear your case. Don't worry. I'll be fair."

"You didn't have to arrest us," David said. "You know good and well that the artifact was planted in Richard's belongings. Yet you've got us caged up in here like we're animals."

Fullerton tipped his cap. "Have a nice evening, gentlemen. See you tomorrow in court."

Reginald narrowed his eyes as he stared back at his two prisoners. "If the monkey comes, there won't be any keys for him to get for you." He snatched the keys off the hook and pocketed them before gesturing for Fullerton to exit first. Moments later, the two gentlemen disappeared outside as the door slammed shut behind them. The sound of the deadbolt clicking into place echoed in the cell.

"I'd like to give that magistrate a piece of my mind," David said.

"I think you already did," Richard said. "And I'm certain he wasn't interested in it."

"How can you be so glib about all this? We have no chance of getting out of here any time soon."

"I wouldn't be so sure," Richard said with a shrug. "You never know what can happen."

"Well, that monkey won't be helping us out, that's for sure. Got any other tricks, Dr. Dolittle?"

"Dr. Dolittle? Who on Earth is that?"

David waved dismissively. "He's just an odd character who talks to animals in a children's book I read to my nephew last time I was home. Now unless you have some other special powers you'd like to let me know about, I think we're going to have to rely on our American ingenuity to figure a way out of this jail cell before morning."

Richard and David began to systematically explore every inch of their cage. They shook bars and dug at the loose mortar surrounding the bricks. When that seemed like a dead end, they scanned the two desks covered with scattered papers in search of something that could help them pry open the lock. After that they studied the cots to see if there was anything they could convert into a tool to open the gate.

Every idea started out with promise but ultimately failed to deliver.

"Please tell me you have another idea," David said.

Richard sat in silence, unsure of what he could say that would assuage David's fears, fears that were suddenly mutual. There wasn't any conceivable way out, and Richard hesitated to admit it.

"Well, Mr. Optimist, do you have anything?" David asked.

Richard sighed and shook his head. "I think we're just going to have to—"

The jangling of keys outside the prison doors interrupted him.

"Have to what?" David insisted.

The door flung open, and a familiar-looking woman strode inside.

"I know you," Richard said. "You're Mr. Fullerton's assistant."

She smiled and nodded. "I have a name. It's Maggie."

"Well, Maggie," Richard began, "what brings you down here?"

"I'm freeing the two of you," she said with a wink and smile while jangling the keys in her hand.

"I don't understand," David said.

"You don't have to understand," she said. "You just need to run like Charles Paddock."

Richard chuckled. "I'm afraid that I can only move like that if there's a wild animal chasing me."

"We're in India," Maggie said as she turned the key. "I can arrange that for you if necessary."

"I'm absolutely speechless," David said. "Why would you do such a thing?"

"I saw what happened," she said.

"What do you mean?" Richard asked.

"A German man placed the idol in your bag while you were out with Mr. Fullerton. I saw everything."

"So the Germans were here?" David asked.

She nodded. "There were about a dozen men who came through here a week ago. I don't know what happened to them, but Fullerton disappeared for a few days only to return with one of them."

"And here you are, risking everything for two strangers you've only met once," David said.

She sighed and shook her head. "If you had stayed in jail, the magistrate planned to release you tomorrow on a technicality and the German would've murdered you in the jungle. That was their plan. The whole ordeal would've probably been reported as a mauling by a wild animal, and that would be that. You'd be dead, and no one else would ever know what really happened."

"Thank you," Richard said as he stepped into the office and gave Maggie a hug.

"Yes," David added, "thank you so much. How can we ever repay you for this act of kindness?"

"I already told you," Maggie said. "I want you to run so that this isn't all in vain."

She nodded toward a door in the back that Richard couldn't see while in the cell.

"Should we exit that way?" he asked.

"If you go out through the front, there's a chance someone might see you," she said. "But if you go out the back, you'll go down a narrow alley, and no one will see you."

"Works for me," David said. He hustled over to the woman and shook her hand. "You're an angel."

"If I were an angel, I would've spoken up sooner," she said.

"Better late than never," Richard said.

They grabbed their bags and proper documentation before slipping outside into the cool evening air. Richard stopped and inhaled.

"Come on, Richard," David said. "We don't have time for this. We need to move."

Richard took one last deep breath and broke into a sprint.

CHAPTER 10

July 2, 1922
Kargil, India

WILHELM STEPPED ONTO THE TRAIN PLATFORM AND scanned the surrounding area for the Buddhist follower who was supposed to meet four members Reichswehr unit. After several minutes, Wilhelm finally noticed a man standing off to the side, wearing a saffron robe. He paced back and forth, muttering to himself.

"I think that's our contact," Wilhelm said to Reinhard, pointing toward the man.

"Are you sure?" Reinhard asked. "He looks a little strange to me."

"Go ask him if he knows Erden," Wilhelm said. "He was supposed to send us one of his men to lead us to the compound."

"Does that man look trustworthy to you?"

Wilhelm covered his face with his right hand and took a deep breath. "Go talk to him *now*."

Reinhard chatted with the man for a couple minutes before returning to Wilhelm.

"So, what did he say?" Wilhelm asked.

"He said he'll take us to Erden."

Wilhelm motioned for the rest of the soldiers to join

them as they strode toward the man. Once all the other soldiers arrived, the Buddhist monk spread his arms wide and grinned, introducing himself as Bankei.

"Welcome to Kargil," he said. "I will take you to Erden, but I need to know that you come on a mission of peace."

"Of course," Wilhelm said. "That is why we're here. Our nation's past history has been one of intense war, and I feel the need to address this within my own soul before I can be an ambassador of peace among my countrymen."

"You've come to the right place," the monk said. "We will unburden your soul and enlighten your mind. Follow me."

The monk strolled leisurely along the street, stopping at random intervals to take deep breaths with his eyes closed. Wilhelm was confused by the monk's behavior, wondering if he was suffering from some sort of disease.

"Are you all right?" Wilhelm asked.

With eyes still shut, the monk nodded. "I'm aligning my spirit."

"With what?"

"The universe," the monk responded. "This is something you will learn how to do soon enough."

Wilhelm furrowed his brow and shot a glance at Reinhard, who shrugged and kept walking. Despite the monk's strange antics, he eventually led them to the monastery situated on a rocky ridge overlooking the city. After he knocked, someone from inside unlatched the gate and swung it open, revealing men in robes gliding back and forth across a courtyard. The common area was decorated with well-manicured bushes and trees, providing for an orderly and neat appearance.

While Erden was known for his teaching of *anatman*, he was also allegedly the monk who knew where all of India's grandest treasures were hidden. During the Reichswehr's previous mission to Egypt, Wilhelm had met a man one evening at a hotel bar in Cairo who was adamant that Erden had been appointed to be the keeper of these secrets for the Buddhists. Wilhelm was reluctant to believe the stranger, but a subsequent conversation with General Seeckt revealed that he had also heard the same story and encouraged Wilhelm to investigate. A trip to China awaited the Reichswehr unit after this assignment, but Wilhelm assured his *wolfsrudel* that they would leave no stone unturned during their time in India.

Erden emerged from around a corner. He remained somber as he approached his guests, bowing his head toward each man.

"Thank you so much for meeting with us," Wilhelm said. "At first, I thought it would be just me who wanted to hear your exposition of the *anatman*. But after sharing with several of my fellow unit members what we were doing, some of them asked if they could join me. Will that be all right with you?"

Erden nodded and gestured for everyone to follow him, still remaining silent.

When they reached a private room, Erden waited until everyone was inside before lighting incense and taking a seat on the floor. He crossed his legs and closed his eyes.

Wilhelm glanced around at the Reichswehr unit and the two other men asked to accompany them. They all started to follow Erden's lead one by one with Wilhelm the last to join. After a few moments of silence, Erden sighed loudly and asked everyone to open their eyes. Then Erden began sharing about *anatman*.

Erden's explanation lasted for nearly half an hour before he asked Wilhelm if they wanted to take a break.

"That would be nice," Wilhelm said. "Plus, there are some other things I'd like to ask you about before you resume."

"What would you like to ask me?"

"Well, I know how this might sound, but I have to ask it."

Erden smiled. "Ask me anything."

Wilhelm stroked his chin. "I have it on good authority that you know where all of India's greatest treasures are hidden. You were chosen because you aren't allowed to accumulate great wealth and would never be tempted to do so."

"Where did you hear such a thing?"

"You're not denying it?" Wilhelm asked. "And pick your words carefully. I know you're not permitted to lie."

"Just because I might know something doesn't mean that I'd ever be obligated to tell you."

Wilhelm nodded subtly. "So, it is true. You know where all the secrets are buried."

"That's actually not entirely true," Erden said. "I don't know where all the treasures are, but I'm the only one who knows the identity of each keeper."

"Well, I don't want them all—just one," Wilhelm said as he dug into his pocket and flicked open his blade. He pointed the tip toward Erden.

"That won't be necessary to coerce me," Erden said. "Or at least, it won't be useful. In my discipline training, I learned how to withstand an immense amount of pain. And no matter what you do with that knife, I won't say a word."

Wilhelm gestured for Reinhard and the others to join the conversation with Erden. "Our favorite monk just warned me that no matter what we do, he won't relinquish the names and locations of the men who know where all the treasures are hidden, including the one we're after."

"Nothing you can say or do will make me tell you what you want to know," Erden said. "Now, I think it's time for you to leave." He pointed toward the door.

"You've made one big mistake," Wilhelm said as a grin eased across his face. "In the midst of your wonderful monastery to protect you from the outside world, you thought this was all about you. But it's not. I know where your mother is. And right now, there are a handful of my agents just waiting to act once I give them the word. I promise you, there won't be much left of her when they're finished with her."

"You're bluffing," Erden said.

"Feel free to take that risk, but it's up to you."

Erden sighed and paced around for a few moments before turning and facing Wilhelm.

"Are you ready to tell me what I want to know?" Wilhelm asked.

Erden nodded. "What treasure do you seek?"

"The raja's treasure hidden in the castle at Jaipur."

Erden's eyes widened. "You won't be able to find it even if you knew where it was. That fortress is guarded every hour of the day by soldiers who patrol the area, making sure visitors don't leave with souvenirs. The chances of being able to get inside to retrieve the treasure will be challenging enough, but then you'll have to find a way to get it out. You will need more than good luck to pull off such a feat."

"I view such obstacles as something that will make my eventual triumph that much more satisfying. Now, I'm going to need that name now."

"How do I know you'll keep your word and not harm my mother?" Erden asked.

"Trust, my friend."

"I trust no one who threatens my family."

Wilhelm patted Erden on the back. "Then I guess this will have to be a first. Because if I come back and discover that you lied, you won't live to regret it. Are you clear about what my intentions are should you attempt to mislead us?"

Erden nodded.

"The name, please," Wilhelm said, gesturing with his hand for Erden to give up.

"Dalir Abbasi."

"And where would I find this Mr. Abbasi? At a monastery like you?"

Erden shook his head. "You'll find him at the market in Torkham, Afghanistan. He's an art seller. Now, please leave. I don't ever want to see your faces in here again."

Wilhelm nodded, a small gesture of appreciation that was met with a sneer from Erden.

"Thank you for your time," Wilhelm said. "You've been most helpful."

CHAPTER 11

Simla, India

THE RETURN TO SIMLA FELT DEFEATING TO RICHARD. After traipsing across the country following their brush with the rogue magistrate, Richard was tired and wondered if they would always be chasing a moving target. The Reichswehr unit had demonstrated it was resourceful in being able to secure the proper documents needed to move about the country and were doing just that at a surprising pace. Meanwhile, their ultimate destination remained a mystery.

Richard and David entered Harvey Carrington's manor and collapsed into chairs in the library while they awaited his appearance. After several minutes, he entered the room, carrying a cup of tea in one hand and a neatly folded newspaper in the other.

"What happened to you two?" Harvey asked, settling into a chair across from the two agents. "You look like you got into a nasty scrap with a couple of tigers."

"That good?" David asked as a glint of a smile flickered across his lips.

"This is what you look like after riding in a third class carriage on an Indian train," Richard said. "However, next time, if you'd like to spring for the extra cost to put us in first class—"

Harvey held up his hand. "I know I may look like I'm made of money, but this is the U.S. Army's money, and unfortunately the budget they gave me is tight. Now, you obviously didn't apprehend the Reichswehr troop, so tell me what happened as well as the real reason you look so dreadful."

Richard and David proceeded to divulge all the details of their dead end with the uncooperative British magistrate as well as their escape. They explained how they needed two days to get out of Maredumilli and return to the more modern section of India before getting train tickets to return to Simla.

Harvey sipped his tea before setting it down on the table next to his chair. "I'm glad you were able to make it back so quickly, because we received some news yesterday about the Reichswehr soldiers' whereabouts."

Richard leaned forward. "They're still in India?"

Harvey nodded. "Fortunately, they haven't left quite yet, though we're still in the dark regarding whether they've obtained what they came for."

"Where are they?" David asked.

"They were last seen headed toward Kargil, which is a long trek north of here," Harvey said. "But fortunately, you'll be able to access it directly by train."

"With first class tickets?" Richard asked.

Harvey sighed and shook his head. "You'll have to figure out a way to upgrade yourselves. Otherwise, it's third class for you—and I was lucky enough to secure those passes. The train is packed all week according to the ticket salesman I spoke with earlier today. Apparently, there's some festival taking place in Kargil, and everyone is headed there."

"And who were the Germans looking for?" David asked.

"A monk by the name of Erden."

* * *

AT THE TRAIN STATION, RICHARD CONTEMPLATED SLEEPING on a bench, a thought that was dismissed when he noticed a woman struggling to lug her bags across the platform.

"Would you like some help?" he asked.

She glanced up at him and smiled. "I'd appreciate that. The men ask for a tip first before they make any attempt to assist you. It's one of the things about this country that I'm not so fond of."

"I'm afraid chivalry is teetering on its last leg in our society," he said. "But I'll happily do what I can to help prop it up."

"Where are you from?" she asked.

"I'm from the United States."

"That much is obvious," she said with a soft laugh. "What part?"

"The south, ma'am. I'm from Memphis, Tennessee."

She nodded. "That would explain it. All the southern gentlemen I've ever met always go out of their way to help me."

"Perhaps it's your infectious smile," Richard said. "You've already lifted my spirits, and I've barely spoken with you for a minute."

She waved him off dismissively. "You're making me blush, Mr. . . ."

"Halliburton. Richard Halliburton."

"I'm Helen Turner."

"It's a pleasure to meet you."

"And what is it that you do, Mr. Halliburton, that has you on the other side of the world and away from Memphis?"

"I'm a travel writer. And what about you? Why are you carrying all this luggage by yourself? Surely, you're not alone."

Helen looked skyward and exhaled slowly. "I'm not alone, but it feels like that most of the time. I'm a government widow, though I'm by myself this time because I simply can't take the sweltering heat anymore. I need to cool off."

"Correct me if I'm wrong, but Kargil isn't exactly mild right now."

"Yes, but it's slightly cooler than here without all the humidity."

The train's brakes hissed as it pulled into the station.

"Will you be joining me in the first class carriage?" she asked.

Richard shook his head. "Unfortunately, I'm stuck in the back, just happy to be on board."

"Would you like to use my husband's ticket?" she asked. "He was planning on coming with me but canceled because of work."

"And you decided to go anyway?"

"Like I said, I must escape the heat—with or without him."

"In that case, I'll accept your generous offer and accompany you for your trip."

Helen placed her purse on top of one of her bags and rummaged through the deep pockets. A few seconds later, she produced the coveted first class ticket.

"This is for you," she said, "though I must admit that this might be more of a treat for me than for you. I just love listening to you southerners talk."

"I'll be happy to entertain you," Richard said. "But I'd just as well listen too. Who knows? Maybe you'll make it in one of my books one day."

David sauntered over to Richard and Helen as the conductor began collecting tickets.

"I believe it's time to board," David said.

Richard nodded. "Indeed it is. And this wonderful woman right here invited me to sit with her in first class."

Richard introduced David and Helen before helping load her suitcases onto the train. David sneered at Richard, who responded with a wry smile.

Once they boarded, Richard didn't get much of a chance to showcase his smooth voice due to Helen's chatty nature. She claimed to be quite knowledgeable about Kargil, and Richard took full advantage, inquiring about the city to help him get a better idea of the layout and consider where the Germans might be headed. He also took a much-needed nap.

When they reached the station in Kargil, Richard assisted Helen in unloading and bid her farewell before waiting for David to emerge from the third class cabin. Fifteen minutes passed before Richard rejoined his fellow agent.

"How was your trip?" Richard asked, a smile already leaking across his lips.

"I hate you," David said. "I'm sure you already know that, but I really hate you."

"That good, huh?"

"The guy next to me held a cage in his lap for his two chickens. Then there were three screaming babies and a kid playing a flute for probably the first time in his life. So, yeah, I hate you."

Richard couldn't suppress a smile. "Why don't I buy you a drink?"

"A single drink isn't going to make up for what I just endured while you rode in first class. I think you'll owe me til the end of time."

Richard winked at his colleague. "I'm sure I'll come up with a more appropriate amount of restitution, but in the meantime, let's go sit down and get our bearings before seeking out this monk."

David agreed to the proposal, and the two found a nearby bar where they could ask around about the monastery. After the first drink, a man seated two chairs away perked up when he heard Richard and David discussing the monastery.

"I'm familiar with many of the Buddhist monasteries here," the man said in a thick British accent. "Maybe it's something I can help you with."

"I don't know the name of it," Richard said. "Are there multiple ones in Kargil?"

"There are two. A relatively new one located just off the central market, while the other one is older and sits on the outskirts of the city."

"Definitely the older one," Richard said. "We'll go there first."

"Anyone in particular you're trying to reach?"

David shook his head. "Just need to talk with some people there."

"Very well then," the man said as he scratched directions onto a napkin. "Good luck in your search."

Richard pocketed the napkin before snatching up the bill. He told the bartender that he wanted to buy the friendly man's last drink as well.

"There's no need to do that," the man said, waving off Richard. "It's my pleasure to help you."

"I insist," Richard said as he pulled out a coin and flipped it up in the air. He slapped his hand on top of the silver piece and patted the man on the back before leaving.

David waited until they were outside before he spoke. "The purpose of traveling as Army Intelligence officers is to gather information and be as forgettable as possible. Showy displays of generosity aren't going to help us be next to invisible."

"Well, I never received that lecture in my training," Richard said, "and neither am I going to stop being a decent human being."

"I'm not asking you to stop that. I'm asking you to be a better agent, one who's more incognito."

Richard stopped and furrowed his brow, studying David intently. "You act as if the two can't co-exist."

"Never mind," David said. "At least you didn't divulge the name of the monk we're looking for."

"I'm sharper than you give me credit for," Richard said.

"Probably because you just had a more comfortable ride in first class."

"You're not going to let that go, are you?"

"Never," David said. "Now, let's get a move on."

The two men wandered through the middle of the city until they ventured down the road leading to the monastery, per the kind man's instructions. And just as he described, they found the compound after a ten-minute walk.

When they approached the entrance, they found it shut. Richard strode up to the guard hut just outside and knocked on it. After a few seconds when no one answered, Richard shielded the glare from the fading sunset reflected on the glass and eased closer.

"There's no one inside," Richard announced.

"Maybe it's time for evening prayers," David said. "Or whatever rituals Buddhists have."

"You mean the *Tam Wat Yen*?"

"The Tam what?"

"The Tam Wat Yen," Richard said. "The name of the evening prayer for Buddhists."

"Well, I had no idea you were so versed on the traditions of Buddhism."

Richard shrugged. "What can I say? I like to read. But

that still doesn't get us inside, does it?"

"Any other ideas, Mr. Well Rested First Class Traveler?"

Richard turned and noticed a man pushing a wooden cart near them. He came to a brief stop and Richard seized his opportunity to query the man.

"Excuse me, sir," Richard said. "Do you happen to know why the gate is closed?"

"It's been closed all day," the man said.

"Do you happen to know why?"

"No one will say," he replied as he resumed his walk down the dusty road.

Richard eased up to the gate as he heard footsteps approaching. "Is anyone in there?"

The sound of a bolt sliding out of place made Richard take a few steps backward as he glanced over at his fellow agent. David's eyes widened as he also awaited someone to step from behind the large door.

"May I help you gentlemen?" asked an elderly man clad in a saffron robe.

"We were hoping to speak with one of your monks," Richard said.

"I'm sorry, but we're all in mourning right now and cannot be disturbed," he said as he walked back inside.

"It's really important," Richard said. "The monk's name is Erden."

The monk stopped and turned slowly toward his two visitors.

"That's the brother we're mourning for," he said as he closed the door.

CHAPTER 12

RICHARD AND DAVID RETURNED TO THE MONASTERY the next morning to inquire again about Erden. A visit to the police station the evening before had proved fruitless as an officer there explained that natural causes was determined to be the reason for the monk's death and that they wouldn't be investigating further. But the two Army Intelligence agents weren't convinced.

After they waited for a few minutes, a monk opened the gate and welcomed them inside. He ushered them to the main office to meet with the abbot, Daifu Jamyang.

Daifu welcomed his surprise guests inside and invited them to sit down on the floor with him. Richard and David removed their shoes and complied.

"As you might well imagine, this is a difficult time for us," Daifu said. "Erden was a beloved brother and an important part of our community here. We're all still in shock over what happened, especially since he was only thirty-six."

"Our condolences to you," Richard said as he nodded solemnly. "It's never easy to make sense of death when someone is taken from us earlier than expected."

"You have experience with this?" Daifu asked.

"I lost my brother a few years ago when he was still young and full of life. It took me a few years to make peace with his death. And I still miss him terribly."

"But you found a way, as will we," Daifu said. "What exactly is the reason for your interest in Erden? Did you know him before he joined the monastery here?"

David shook his head. "We never met him. However, we're looking for a group of men, a group that we believe Erden met with right before he died. And we think they might be the ones responsible for his death."

"But Erden died in his sleep," Daifu said. "There was nothing suspicious about how his life ended. He simply didn't wake up one morning."

"Did he have a history of good health?" Richard asked.

"As far as I know, he was in outstanding health. He was always one of our more diligent workers in the garden, tirelessly pulling weeds and tending the crops. I'm convinced the reason we had a greater yield over the past two years was because of his involvement there."

"With all due respect, men who are in good health don't just die in their sleep at such a young age," David said.

"What other way is there to explain it?" the abbot asked. "No one enters through our gates without us knowing about it. And there wasn't anyone else inside that night other than the monks."

"Are you sure about that?" Richard asked.

"Yes," Daifu answered. "We must take careful note of who enters our monastery."

"Why is that? Have you had people attempt to kill some of the monks before?" David asked.

"Absolutely not, but we have had incidents where people sought to harm our brothers in other ways. The intent was never to kill but certainly to embarrass or shame the men here. So we decided to take measures to prevent such events from happening again."

Richard sighed and looked out the window into the courtyard. "Yet something happened to him, right here, inside these walls."

"That's what you're claiming," the abbot said. "We're satisfied that he simply died in his sleep."

"But what if he didn't?" Richard asked. "What if there's a murderer lurking in your midst? What then?"

"I would want to extract that person from our sacred community," Daifu said. "We have no place for violent behavior among us."

"At least let us help you," David said.

Daifu took a step back and stroked his chin as he stared at his visitors. "Why is this so important to you?"

"Look, I understand what you're going through as a community," Richard began. "It's not easy, but there's something bigger at stake here. We believe there's a group of German special agents seeking to enrich their coffers to go to war again very soon. And we suspect that Erden somehow knew something that they needed know. I'm even more convinced of that since he's passed away. They wouldn't kill him unless they felt threatened by him or feared that he might tell someone about the nature of their visit. I'm betting it was the latter."

Daifu steepled his fingers and pressed them gently against his lips. He closed his eyes and remained silent for a few moments.

"That type of inquiry might upset the men," Daifu said. "They are still very upset as Erden was beloved by all."

But Richard continued to press Daifu. "Is avoiding momentary pain a worthy sacrifice if it helps put a stop to the Germans' ambitions of another war?"

"You're a wise man," the abbot said. "I will allow it, but only for the next three hours. This doesn't need to be drawn out. Ask your questions and then leave, for the good of our souls so we can mourn again."

Richard and David affirmed their intent to work swiftly and delicately before Daifu assigned them an escort while they remained in the compound.

During the first hour, they split up to interview a number of monks who worked with Erden on certain projects outside the monastery walls. However, nothing seemed to make Erden particularly important to the Germans. When Richard and David took a break, they discussed what they'd learned, which wasn't much.

"So far, I don't have anything that makes sense as to why Wilhelm would want to track down this monk," Richard said.

"But the fact that the Reichswehr unit was here and now Erden is dead is reason enough to believe that he was important in some way."

"We just don't know how—and that's the problem."

As Richard and David prepared to return to the interviews, Daifu wore a furrowed brow as he approached them.

"What is it?" Richard asked. "Is everything okay?"

"I'm afraid you've upset some of the men," the abbot said. "We have a festival to prepare for tomorrow, and some of the other monks have asked to forego your inquiries as they want to make sure they finish their other duties on time."

"Can we come back another time?" David asked.

"I'm sorry, but I need to ask you to leave."

"But we were just getting started," David protested. "I thought you wanted justice for Erden. I thought you didn't want to be responsible for aiding these men who are determined to start another war."

"That's not my role in this world," Daifu said. "And I don't wish to discuss this any further with you."

Two bulkier monks strode up beside Diafu, flanking him on each side. The subtle message was clear.

"Thank you for your time and for opening up your monastery to us," Richard said. "We'll figure out another way to stop those men and get answers regarding Erden's death."

"May you be well," Daifu said.

David didn't move until Richard grabbed his fellow agent's arm and tugged him toward the gate.

"He's not changing his mind," Richard whispered. "Let's go."

With the two monks enforcing Daifu's wishes, Richard and David exited the compound. They stopped and watched the gate slowly swing shut, listening as the iron latch fell into place. David kicked at the dirt and let out a string of expletives.

"Now we're at the mercy of someone seeing those Germans and reporting it to someone who gets the word back to Army Intelligence," David said. "And it takes an enormous amount of luck for that to happen."

"It's not out of the realm of possibility."

David shook his head and pursed his lips. "Even if the stars aligned for us, by the time we found out about it, the Reichswehr unit would've had time to disappear again. I feel like we're chasing a ghost across this godforsaken country."

"Well, what do you want to do now?" Richard asked. "Want to get on a train tomorrow and return to Simla to deliver the good news to Harvey in person?"

"Let's hold off on that," David said. "I'm tired and need a drink."

* * *

LATER THAT EVENING, RICHARD AND DAVID FOUND A SMALL English-style pub three blocks from their hotel. Richard swilled his ginger beer, while David polished off his second pint. The two men continued to speculate on what it was that Wilhelm wanted with Erden, though neither of the agents could conceive of an idea that made sense.

"It just seems so random," Richard said. "At this point, the only thing that we know is that Wilhelm knew we were following him and wanted to throw us off his trail."

David shrugged. "Maybe that's it, though didn't he send one of his men to kill you? How would he even know if you're alive or not, especially since you threw him overboard in the middle of a storm? There's no way he survived that."

"I don't know. There was a German in Maredumilli. It could be him. Or there could've been a rendezvous location for the assassin from the *Gold Shell* to report the outcome, and if he never made it there, that could've signaled that I was still alive."

David stared at his empty glass. "We're just guessing right now. The truth is we know little more than we did before we came here. At best, we've lost several more days in tracking them down."

"Speaking of which, we need to get back to our hotel and get to bed," Richard said. "Our train leaves at 7:00a.m. tomorrow, and I want to be well rested for the ride seeing that I haven't met any generous benefactors to grant me a first class ticket."

"You're probably right," David said as he stood and slid his chair beneath their table.

Once the two agents left the pub, they walked a block before a man tapped Richard on the shoulder. He spun around to see a man clad in a saffron robe. David, who had continued walking, hustled back to rejoin Richard.

"What do you want?" Richard asked. "Were you friends with Erden?"

The monk nodded. "I'm the one who convinced him to join the monastery. I thought it would be a safe place for him."

Richard furrowed his brow. "A safe place? Was he in danger?"

"Yes," the monk said. "He knew too much—and I knew eventually it would catch up with him."

"Knew too much about what?" David asked.

"Our country's greatest secrets. He was chosen to be the guardian of all of India's wealth, keeping it safe from the British."

"Was this some kind of order?" Richard asked.

The monk nodded. "It was established long ago when the British first came here and began to colonize India. The leaders were powerless to stop the English from ruling, but they created a group called Abhib, short for *abhibhaavak*. It means *guardian* in Hindi."

"And Erden was chosen?" Richard asked.

"Years ago, his grandfather became the first guardian and passed the duties along to his son and then Erden. He never told me everything he knew, but he explained once that instead of writing down where all the wealth was stored, there were individuals dispersed all across the world who knew where a single treasure was hidden. However, Erden was responsible for knowing where each one of those people were when the British were finally expelled from our country."

"So the identities of their locations died with him?" David asked.

"There are two other guardians, but the information has never been written down. The leaders at the time deemed it better that way in order to protect that list from ever falling into the wrong hands."

"It might be a little too late for that now," Richard said. "Is there anything you can help us with?"

The monk nodded. "I share a room with Erden—and I also shared his secret. He knew he was dying in the middle of the night. I woke up to try to help him."

"Why didn't you tell anyone this?" David asked.

"I was responsible for bringing Erden into the community," the monk said. "If I told them what I knew, they would've rejected me. Such an offense is an unforgivable one, even within Buddhism."

"What did he say?" Richard asked.

"He told me the location of all the men and made me commit it to memory. And then he told me what the Germans wanted."

"And?" David asked.

"They inquired about a treasure, though Erden didn't tell me which one. He just told me the name of the man the Germans sought. He's Dalir Abbasi, an art dealer in the market in Torkham, Afghanistan."

"Afghanistan," Richard repeated as his eyes widened.

"Yes," the monk said. "They have a few days' head start. You must hurry if you intend to find these men and deal with them accordingly. However, I'm afraid it might be too late."

A train whistle pierced the night sky.

"That train leaves in five minutes," Richard said to David. "And we need to be on it."

"The train won't take you all the way there," the monk said. "You must travel through Khyber Pass to reach Torkham."

"But isn't Khyber Pass forbidden right now?" David asked.

"We'll have to get creative," Richard said.

CHAPTER 13

RICHARD AND DAVID NEEDED FIVE DAYS TO REACH Peshwar, India's last major outpost, before entering the Khyber Pass. During the trip, Richard had managed to snag first-class tickets for himself on all five legs of the journey, while he secured passes for three first-class legs for David. Their conversations ranged from favorite baseball teams to the recovery effort taking place in Europe since the end of the Great War. More than anything, Richard began to develop a deeper appreciation for his colleague and all that he had done since the conflict ended.

Upon reaching Peshwar, the conversation shifted toward their purpose for being there and how they could travel through the Khyber Pass to reach Torkham, Pakistan. Finding an art dealer in a small market seemed simple enough, but getting there the greater—and far more dangerous—challenge, a fact they learned upon speaking with an officer at the military outpost in Peshwar.

Lieutenant Langhari explained that Khyber Pass was the only suitable thoroughfare for automobiles to travel between Afghanistan and Pakistan for hundreds of miles in either direction.

"The thieves living in the mountains have made a sport of robbing tourists and other naïve travelers. When the

British military threatened to lay waste to the pillagers' way of life, they came to the peace table and negotiated a deal. On Tuesdays and Fridays, all vehicles would be left alone, but the other days of the week, anyone traveling along that path is fair game. As a consequence, Tuesdays and Fridays constitute a mad dash along the steep road early in the morning to avoid driving through the sun-baked cliffs in the heat of the day.

"What's the best way to get through?" Richard asked.

"I can take you to Landi Kotal, which is the last Pakistani village before you begin your ascent up Khyber Pass," Langhari said. "I have to check on how our border agents are doing, and you are welcome to join me."

"And then what?" David asked.

"You can't very well hike up the pass. However, you might be able to find someone to let you ride with them for the right price."

"That shouldn't be a problem," David said.

"In that case, I'm leaving in about an hour. Just wait outside the gates here, and I'll be back in a few minutes."

When Langhari returned, he ushered Richard and David to a transport truck, and the three of them crammed inside.

"I'm sorry that this isn't a more comfortable ride," Langhari said.

"We'll manage," David said. "Or at least, I'll manage. I've spent plenty of time riding in third class carriages on trains across the continent, unlike Mr. First Class here."

"Don't act like I'm some sort of English lord," Richard fired back. "I'm just resourceful."

"And conniving," David sniped.

Langhari shook his head. "Getting from one point to another can be challenging no matter how you travel. The fact that you both were able to get this far is a testament to your good fortune and your fortitude."

When they reached Landi Kotal, the officer wished Richard and David good luck as they departed. They found a hostel Langhari had recommended and secured their personal effects before asking around about vehicles that would be traveling over the pass early the next morning.

The mail carrier was the only one who had space in his vehicle, though he wasn't immediately inclined to allow the two agents to join him even with the offer of several pounds.

"It's very hot when we reach the summit," said Fahad as he eyed Richard and David closely. "Just because I have room doesn't mean I should try to fill it with two people."

"I'm pleading with you," Richard said. "Is there anything else I can do to persuade you to take us?"

"*If* I allow this, we must leave well before daybreak tomorrow to avoid the warmest part of the day," Fahad said.

"We'll be here on time, I promise," Richard said.

"Make it three pounds each, and I'll do it."

Richard would've forked over more since there weren't any other options, but he was pleased that Fahad didn't gouge them any more than he did.

* * *

THE RIDE THROUGH KHYBER PASS WAS LONG AND FAR hotter than advertised. Richard and David listened for most of the trip as Fahad delivered passionate soliloquies regarding the English occupation of Pakistan and the history of the treacherous stretch of road they traveled. He pointed out several locations where people were killed by bandits or died when their vehicle careened off the edge. While the stories were entertaining, Richard found himself wondering whether or not they would actually make it to Afghanistan.

"How long have you been driving this route?" Richard asked.

"About three years, " Fahad answered. "I'm one of the more experienced drivers on this route. Most men can't handle the demands of navigating this path each day."

The road narrowed to a one-lane passageway as it curved around a corner, though Fahad maintained his speed.

Richard glanced at David, who was clawing at his seat. Lines creased his forehead as he stared wide-eyed at the scene unfolding through the windshield. Turning toward the front, Richard saw what appeared to frighten David—another cart hurtling toward them with nowhere else to go.

Fahad stomped on the brakes and shifted into reverse.

"Hold on," he said as he began driving backward. Once he reached a spot where the road widened enough to accommodate two vehicles at once, Fahad parked and waited for the oncoming traffic to pass. Once there weren't any more cars, he re-entered the one-lane path.

"Are you sure it's safe to travel this way again?" Richard asked.

"This is why so many drivers quit," Fahad said. "This job isn't for those with a weak constitution."

"You didn't answer my question," Richard said.

"We'll be in Torkham soon enough."

Richard spent the rest of the trip drinking in the view near the top of the pass and praying that another car didn't smash into them head-on whenever the road narrowed. After a couple hours, they finally arrived at the border and entered Pakistan just outside Torkham. Fahad dropped off Richard and David near the center of the city, giving them directions to the market.

Richard and David meandered around the market for a

while, acting as if they were interested in some of the goods being sold there. Eventually, they sauntered up to the area where Fahad told them they'd find the art shop. It was open, but there was nobody inside.

The woman in the booth across from them eyed them carefully.

"Are you interested in purchasing something?" she asked as she walked across the aisle separating the two businesses.

"Perhaps you can help us," Richard said. "We're looking for Dalir Abassi. Have you seen him today?"

The woman shook her head. "He's been gone for five days now. We're all very worried that something happened to him."

"Did you see anyone stop by here and talk with him?" David asked.

"The last time I saw him, a couple men came by and asked him a few questions. He didn't look happy, but he left with them and asked me to watch his store while he was gone. I haven't seen him since."

"Do you know where he lives?" Richard asked as he waved a pound note in front of her face.

She nodded and smiled. "I'll take you there in a half hour when we close for lunch."

When lunchtime arrived, the woman escorted Richard and David to Abassi's house located less than a five-minute walk from the market. Situated on the ground floor of a two-story complex, the home was cozy and decorated with an array of Afghani art. The layout was open with the kitchen, living area, and dining area all in one spot. There was a toilet with a bathtub and two other rooms, one being Abassi's bedroom while the other was a study.

"May I ask what your interest is in Dalir?" the woman asked.

"We want to know about the men who visited him," Richard said. "We believe they're very dangerous, and we need to speak with them."

"I doubt they're still here," she said. "Someone would've told me by now. Everyone around the market has been worried about Dalir."

Richard and David searched for a half hour and couldn't come up with any actionable lead on where Dalir Abassi might have directed the Germans.

"I need to return to my store," the woman said. "And I need to ask you to please leave now. You haven't found anything, and I don't feel comfortable letting you stay here any longer."

Richard offered the woman another pound, but she shook her head.

"I won't ask again."

Richard was about to leave when he spun around and hustled over to Abassi's desk. Pulling open the drawer, Richard tapped the bottom of it, which emitted a hollow sound.

"Find something?" David asked.

"Now," the woman said as she narrowed her eyes at Richard.

He refused to look at her, ignoring her pleas while investigating the clue he thought he'd found. After several seconds, he found a latch on the side that released the top portion of the drawer and revealed a hidden chamber beneath.

"Would you look at this?" Richard asked.

Inside was a weathered map of the region with only one location circled.

"Are you thinking what I'm thinking?" David asked.

Richard nodded. "That's got to be where the treasure is."

"Please return Dalir's possessions to his drawer and come with me right now, or else I will go get the authorities," she said.

"Coming," Richard said, replacing everything but the map in the drawer and then reassembling all the pieces.

Richard and David hustled outside, thanking the woman profusely as she pulled the door shut and gestured for them to walk in front of her back to the market.

"Thank you for your help," Richard said.

"I hope what you found helps you bring Dalir back to us," she said. "We all miss him."

Richard and David waved goodbye as they peeled off onto a side street.

"Well, at least we know where we're going next," Richard said.

"It's still a guess," David warned. "Just playing devil's advocate here, but that could be a family heirloom of sorts or hold some other sentimental value to him."

"Not hidden like that," Richard said.

"If you're wrong, we may give the Reichswehr unit an insurmountable head start that may ultimately cost us our ability to capture them."

"I'm not concerned with that at the moment," Richard said. "Right now, we just need to figure out the fastest way to Jaipur, India."

CHAPTER 14

Jaipure, India

RICHARD AND DAVID HAD TO BRIBE THEIR WAY BACK to India, burning through a substantial amount of funds in the process. After finding a man willing to make a late afternoon run back through Khyber Pass, they found a produce truck heading to Peshwar and used the railway to finally arrive in Jaipur three days later. They checked into a hostel, and Richard collapsed on the bed.

"I'm convinced the only way to travel is in first class," he said.

"How do the paupers do it?" David asked, needling Richard. "It's difficult to believe they are tougher than a trained spy who travels the world as a profession."

"I *can* do it, but it's not my preference."

David chuckled. "Well, you better get up because we don't have time to lay around with the Reichswehr out there. They have a big jump on us, and for all we know, they might already have absconded with the treasure."

Just outside their window, a goat bleated, followed by the cackling of hens. Richard scrambled to his feet and peered into the courtyard, which apparently doubled as the hostel owner's barnyard.

Richard closed the window and then rubbed his face with

his hands. "Can't I at least shave? I feel like I'm turning into an actual vagabond."

David sighed. "Make it snappy. We've got a lot of ground to cover."

After Richard freshened up and removed his three-day scruff, he joined David outside. They started their search by canvassing the area near Fort Jaighr, which was the supposed location of one of India's most infamous treasures. To the two agents, that seemed like the most logical place to begin.

For a couple hours, they entered local hostels and restaurants and asked the staff and other regular patrons if anyone had happened to see a small group of men with German accents. However, each business led to a constant refrain of customers and employees alike shaking their heads and shrugging. With each failed attempt to find someone who'd seen any members of the Reichswehr unit, Richard grew more frustrated.

"Why don't we just go up to the fort and see if we can find them?" he suggested after questioning the last person in a pub. "It'll be better than wasting our time around here."

David looked at his watch. "The fort closes in half an hour, and it'll take us longer than that to make it up there. We'll go first thing in the morning."

Satisfied with the change in tactics, Richard nodded and returned to the hostel with David before the two men fell asleep.

* * *

ADVIK, THE INDIAN MAN TENDING THE BAR, GLANCED AT THE piece of paper his brother gave him before sliding him a few coins and winking at him. Once things slowed down a bit,

Advik asked his boss if he could take a short break. Upon getting approval to step out for a few minutes, Advik raced down a back alley and hustled up a flight of steps where the German man had told him to go.

"What is it, Advik?" Hans Reinhard asked after answering the door.

"They were just here," the Indian man said.

"Who? The Americans?"

Advik nodded. "There were two men, and they were asking everyone about you."

"What did you tell them?" Reinhard asked.

"The same as everyone else: that we haven't ever seen any Germans in our city and that we wouldn't forget them if we did."

"And where did they go?"

Advik handed Reinhard a piece of paper with the address scribbled on it. Reinhard dug into his pocket and passed Advik a handful of coins.

"That should cover it," Reinhard said. "Thank you for this."

* * *

RICHARD BOLTED UPRIGHT IN BED AND LOOKED AT HIS watch. It was just past 2:00 a.m., and he sensed something was wrong. With goats bleating in the courtyard, he eased over toward the window and slowly drew back the drapes to see if he could detect any movement. As he did, he saw a chicken skittering away from one of the goats.

Richard rushed across the room and shook David. "We've gotta move. They're here."

"The Reichswehr team?" David asked.

"Yes, now get your shoes on and grab your gun. We need to be ready for them."

"Did you see them?"

"No, not exactly," Richard said. "But I've got a feeling they're out there."

"Maybe they're just trying to frighten us to come out of our room to confirm it's us."

Richard eyed David closely. "Is that a chance you're willing to take? Now grab your gun, and let's get going."

Once they were both ready, David grabbed Richard's bicep. "What's your plan?"

"We're going to run."

"That's not a plan—that's an escape strategy."

"Fine," Richard said. "Let's use the railing for the stairs to get up onto the roof. We'll have an advantage up there."

David nodded. "Lead the way."

Richard eased the door open and peeked through the crack. Satisfied that the steps leading to their room were clear, he yanked the door open. Before he could get any farther, a Reichswehr agent slammed into Richard, hitting him first with a body blow followed with a swift kick to his chest. Richard staggered into the room and fell onto his back.

The operative pounced on top of Richard and raised a knife to kill him. At the same time, another Reichswehr agent burst into the room, also wielding a knife. However, both men froze when the click of a gun echoed off the walls.

"I wouldn't do that if I were you," David said.

The German on top of Richard slowly stood with hands raised, still clutching a knife.

"Place the knife on the table," David ordered, gesturing with the barrel of his weapon. "Both of you."

The man put his blade down with his right hand, while keeping his left hand raised. However, before he let go of his dagger completely, he whipped it toward David and dove aside. David dodged the knife and took aim at the German. But the gun jammed.

Richard went on the offensive, punching the closest agent in the face. He staggered backward but spun around and exited the room. In an instant, Richard followed them as they scrambled toward the roof of the hostel. The first agent climbed up and reached down to help his colleague. But Richard latched onto the man's leg and pulled downward.

Caught in a human tug-of-war, the agent thrashed his foot back and forth, kicking Richard in the face. But his grip held fast. Moments later, David rushed outside and started tugging on the agent's other leg. Richard could feel the man inching toward them as his grip slipped.

The man on the roof squatted before yanking upward again to gain more leverage. When that strategy failed, he reached in his pocket with his right hand and pulled out his knife before hurling it at David.

The blade slashed David's bicep and fell to the ground. David instinctively reached for the cut as he groaned. When he did, he let go of the agent's leg, allowing the German on the roof to pull his fellow soldier to safety.

Richard didn't hesitate to pursue the two men, scrambling up onto the roof after them. However, instead of running away, both Reichswehr unit members crouched low and prepared to strike. Glancing over his shoulder, Richard saw David fighting through the pain and trying to climb up.

One of the German's gestured for Richard to engage. However, he hesitated as David struggled to join the fracas on the roof.

Not wanting to lose the men and knowing that they were unarmed, Richard made a run at them. He recalled his training from Dr. Knapp and began to fight with the nearest

Reichswehr agent. They traded punches before the other agent assisted, forming a double team against Richard.

As he struggled to land a knockout blow, one of the agents put him in a headlock.

"This is the end of the line, Mr. Halliburton," the agent said. "You have overstepped your bounds for the last time."

Richard strained to see over the edge to locate David, whose hand was soaked in blood. He grimaced as he peered up toward Richard.

"I'm sorry," David mouthed.

Richard looked back toward the other agent, who was smiling satisfactorily. "It's over."

CHAPTER 15

RICHARD TRIED TO RESIST THE GERMAN, BUT THE hold was too tight. Despite struggling to break free, Richard realized his brash dash onto the roof was a mistake that he was about to pay for with his life. He thrashed back and forth until the two men subdued him with their death grip. Closing his eyes, Richard prepared to accept his fate.

He wondered if he'd hear his neck crack seconds before he died. Instead, he heard another kind of crack.

A gunshot ripped through the night air, setting off a flurry of activity in the makeshift barnyard below and among residents in the surrounding area. Richard didn't move as he felt the hands of one of the men drop off.

Then another shot followed by the remaining agent slumping to the ground in a heap.

Richard opened his eyes slowly, hoping that he wasn't next. Instead, the hostel owner was standing in front of Richard, wearing a big grin.

"It's safe now."

Richard glanced down at David, who was tending his shoulder while leaning against the handrail below.

"How did you know?" Richard stammered as he directed his attention toward the armed owner.

"I saw those men earlier," the owner said. "I knew they were trouble."

"Thank you," Richard said. "You have no idea how much trouble they are."

Richard and the man both ignored the buzz from the neighbors calling out to find out what happened.

"Are you all right?" the man asked Richard.

"I think so, but I know my colleague isn't."

Richard eased off the roof and jumped onto the steps in front of their room. He knelt down and helped David stop the bleeding. The owner joined them moments later.

"Do you need medical attention?" he asked.

"I think I'll live," David said. "I just couldn't get up onto the roof with my arm bleeding like that. My grip strength was gone."

"No need to apologize," Richard said, "especially when we have the Indian Buffalo Bill looking out for us."

The owner grinned. "I read about your wild west in America. It's why I bought a gun and learned to shoot."

Richard smiled and shook his head. "It's probably not like anything you read about, but at the moment, I don't care. You saved my life."

"You get cleaned up. The police are on their way. I'll take care of them."

"Are you sure?" David asked.

"Yes. It's no problem, no problem."

"Thanks," David said.

Richard waited until the owner left before retreating inside the room.

"Well, they're obviously here," Richard said as he helped patch up David's wound.

"Which means they haven't extracted the treasure yet," David added.

"At least we have a chance of beating them to it."

"Yeah, but now we don't have any leads since the gunslinger took them out. I was hoping he'd just frighten them away and we could get them to lead us back to Wilhelm. But no such luck."

"Don't mock the owner," Richard said. "Did you see that grin on his face? He was so proud."

"Maybe we should take him back with us to America. He'd love Colorado."

"Or Wyoming."

"In the meantime, we've got some more pressing issues to handle."

Richard nodded. "Any ideas on how we're going to find Wilhelm?"

"He knows where we're staying," David said.

"But surely he doesn't think we're going to stay here after that attack," Richard said.

"Maybe, but he's going to send someone over here to find out what happened to us," David said. "But I'm not sure that we want to track him back."

"Why not?"

"I think finding that treasure is obviously our priority, at least getting our hands on it before Wilhelm does."

"What do you suggest we do next then?"

"I think we find a new place to stay and do whatever we can to find the treasure before he does."

"You don't think Wilhelm could lead us to the treasure?"

David shook his head. "It's clear that he doesn't have it yet, so I think that would be a waste of our time."

"But we don't know where to start," Richard protested.

David's eyes lit up. "I have an idea. Do you still have that map?"

Richard nodded and dug into his coat pocket. "This only

had the city circled. I don't know why you think you're going to find the exact location on this."

David grabbed a box of matches off the desk in the corner of the room and ignited one stick. Holding it near the map, a series of words came into focus, darkening as the paper heated up.

"Well," Richard said as his eyes widened, "would you look at that?"

CHAPTER 16

THE NEXT MORNING, RICHARD AND DAVID AWOKE IN the private residence of the hostel owner. He had generously offered to hide them away for the remainder of the night so they could get some much needed rest. Before sending his guests out the door, he dug up disguises for them. Decked out in navy-blue *pagris* with stylish white tunics, Richard and David blended in better than they'd imagined as they navigated the streets of Jaipur toward Fort Jaigahr.

Upon arriving at the ancient military installation, they surveyed the outside walls for a few minutes.

"Are you interested in learning more about the fort?" a man asked.

Richard looked around and almost missed the man, who was barely five feet tall. "Of course I would," Richard said. "Do you know much about this place?"

"You're in luck," the man said. "I'm the perfect person to take you through this magnificent place. My father was one of the curators here, and I practically grew up on the grounds of Fort Jaigahr."

Richard gestured forward. "Please lead the way."

The man introduced himself as Vikrant and rubbed his hands together as he gave a brief overview of the fort. He explained its significance in Indian history and what efforts were being taken to preserve that for future generations.

"Come this way," Vikrant said.

He meandered along a path leading inside to the Charbagh garden, which was divided into four quadrants and in full bloom. With a pool located in the center connecting all the sections together, Richard thought it resembled Eden as he imagined it.

Vikrant hopped on top of the ledge of the pool and continued. "Since northern India is drier than the rest of the country, generations of people from this part of the world figured out a long time ago than in order to not just survive but thrive they needed to create a way to capture and store water. The tanks located beneath the fort can store millions of gallons of water."

Richard admired Vikrant's showmanship, acting as if he were leading a crowd of several hundred instead of just two men.

"Any questions?" Vikrant asked.

Richard raised his hand, playing along with Vikrant's oversold spectacle.

"You, sir," he said, pointing at Richard. "You have a question."

Richard nodded. "I've heard several rumors about the water storage as it's related to this fort, and I'm hoping you can either confirm them or put them to rest."

Vikrant jumped down from the pool ledge, landing smoothly on both feet a couple meters away from Richard.

"You're treasure hunters, aren't you?" Vikrant said with a chuckle. "I should've been more perceptive."

"I prefer to think of myself as simply a curious person," Richard said. "If I happen to find a treasure in my adventures, that'd be wonderful. But I'm far more interested in experiencing all the moment has to offer and all the culture and history affiliated with the places I visit so I can share the experience with others."

"So you're a writer?" Vikrant asked.

Richard nodded. "Your deductive skills are quite impressive."

David shifted his weight from one foot to the other. "But can you answer the question?"

Vikrant shot David a look. "Are you in a hurry?"

"You might say that," he said. "We're just interested in getting some of these questions we've had answered so we can determine what next steps we should take."

"Next steps for what?"

"Whether or not we should look for the treasure," David said.

"You're always welcome to search for it. In fact, just the other day, I met some other men from out of town who were looking for—"

"Were they German?" Richard asked.

"Yes, but—"

"Where did you send them?" David asked.

"I didn't send anyone anywhere," Vikrant said while stamping his foot. "I thought you desired a guide, but it's clear that you had ulterior motives. I'm not inclined to waste any more of my time with you."

Richard placed his arm around Vikrant. "We appreciate all the knowledge you shared with us, and we want to learn more about this beautiful piece of architecture. However, we are highly interested in confirming one way or another the true nature of the stories regarding the hidden treasure in this fort."

Vikrant sighed and stared off in the distance for a moment before continuing the conversation with Richard.

David then slipped their guide a couple pounds. He looked down at the money and smiled.

"What exactly do you want to know?" he asked.

David sighed. "Is it possible there's a vast treasure hidden in the collection pools or holding tanks beneath the fort?"

"The collection pools have been drained several times over the years for maintenance purposes," Vikrant said. "They've been repaired, painted, and cleaned, which all seem to happen with striking regularity. So, I would venture to guess that any treasure hidden there would've long since been extracted either by dishonest workers or by the officials in charge of preserving the structure. The holding tanks below, on the other hand, that's another story."

"Can you take us to them?" David asked.

"That area of the fort is forbidden," Vikrant said.

David took out a five-pound note and playfully slapped it against Vikrant's chest. "Just how forbidden of an area is it?"

Vikrant grasped the money and inspected it. He glanced around as if he were checking to make sure no one was watching him.

"Well?" David said.

"Follow me," Vikrant said.

As Richard and David trailed behind their guide, the two Army Intelligence agents spoke in hushed tones with one another.

"Do you still have the paper with the inscription copied from the map?" Richard asked.

David nodded subtly. He dug into his pocket and produced a piece of paper before handing it to Richard, who read the note to himself beneath his breath.

"Falling from heaven and landing below,
Hidden forever and never to flow."

"What is a more appropriate description when it comes to that riddle we found on this map?" David asked. "The holding tanks or the collection pools?"

"At first I thought the collection pools, but that sounds like a dead end," Richard said.

Now silent, they all plodded along a path before descending several flights of stairs. Vikrant ushered them over a rope designed to keep visitors out and guided Richard and David down a dimly lit corridor that was at least fifty meters long.

"I'm curious as to how many holding tanks there are," Richard said. "Ten? Twenty? Fifty? A hundred?"

Vikrant took a hard right and swung open a pair of double doors, revealing a large room with dozens of circular tanks constructed out of stone. Richard estimated they rose about four feet off the ground and were approximately thirty feet in circumference.

"I've never counted them," Vikrant began, "but I've been told they collectively can hold more than twenty-two million liters of water."

Richard's mouth fell agape, first from sheer awe of the size of the space then from the realization that if the treasure were hidden in one of the tanks, it would take quite a while to find it.

"Ready to get to work?" David asked.

Richard wasn't. He was still trying to process not only the incredibly challenging task ahead of him but also wondering how long they had before either Vikrant was discovered or someone else wanted to have his coffers padded. Neither situation was idyllic.

"Did you bring the document in your bag?" David asked.

Richard nodded. "It's right here," he said as he pulled it out and handed it to David.

"We need to study this a bit more," David said as he hustled beneath a skylight in one corner of the room. "We need to find some more clues to make our search easier."

Both men surveyed the document several times, but were unable to come up with anything definitive.

"Did you bring your matches?" Richard asked David.

"You think there's more that we didn't find last time?"

Richard nodded. "Let's try the back."

"There's nothing on the back," David said. "Besides, any hidden messages would've shown up the last time we held a high heat near the paper."

"Just bear with me," Richard said as he struck a match and started to edge it closer to the document. After about a minute, no other markings became visible.

David sighed. "I don't think this is going to work. I'm going to start looking."

Richard and David both froze when they heard the sound of a brick smashing against the cobblestone floor followed by several men's voice speaking quietly.

"Who is that?" Vikrant shouted.

The voice and the subsequent noise ceased. Vikrant hustled in the direction of the sound, frantically searching for the perpetrators. After a cursory glance, he found nothing. David joined him, scanning the room for any sign of where the men were. When David was unable to find something right away, Vikrant shuffled across the room.

Richard returned his attention to the old document and held it near the heat of another match. After several seconds of waving the small flame back and forth beneath the paper, another symbol appeared.

"Vikrant," Richard began, waving his guide over, "what's this?"

"It's a Hindi symbol for a number," Vikrant said.

"*Ashtadash*, which is eighteen in English."

Richard clenched his fists and let out an exuberant shout. "I found it," he said.

"So did I," David yelled back across the room. "Number eighteen, right?"

Richard sprang to his feet and sprinted across the room toward David.

"We did it," Richard said as he skidded to a stop next to his partner and slapped him on the back. They crouched low and eyed the tank carefully, looking for any loose stones or apparent openings. But the structure appeared solidly built.

Richard suddenly noticed the room was eerily quiet. "Where's Vikrant?"

David scanned the room before both men hustled down the aisles, looking for their guide. After a cursory search and repeated calls for him, they rejoined at the tank.

Richard sighed and shook his head. Their diminutive host was nowhere to be seen.

"He's gone," Richard said.

CHAPTER 17

RICHARD AND DAVID DECIDED TO LOOK FOR THE treasure in the tank and worry about Vikrant later. However, Richard stressed the need to work quickly to unearth the fortune and secure it before the Reichswehr unit stumbled on them or worse—Vikrant alerted the Germans.

"Where do you want to start?" David asked.

Richard eyed the structure for a moment. "Let's just check everywhere to see if can find an opening where they might have stashed the jewels."

The tank walls were constructed of stone that was about a foot thick. While the outside seemed like an unlikely place to store the treasure, Richard felt like it was necessary to begin there before diving into the water.

As the two men methodically tried to cajole and jiggle any stones loose, they didn't find any readily apparent opening.

"Ready to get wet?" Richard asked.

David furrowed his brow. "I thought you were the expert swimmer here."

"That doesn't mean I want to get wet for just any reason."

"Well, I still nominate you."

"Fine," Richard said as he rolled up his sleeves. "But I want to know what I'm getting myself into here."

He leaned over the side and reached down into the tank to feel for the bottom. His fingers reached it before the water covered his elbow. Rushing over to the adjacent tank, he plunged his hand inside and repeated the process.

"What is it?" David asked.

"Just as I thought," Richard said as he brought his arm out of the tank. "Tank number eighteen has an elevated bottom."

"Meaning?"

"Meaning that it looks the same from the outside but there's a vast amount of room underneath that could be used to hide any enormous amount of treasure."

"Now we just need to figure out a way to pump the water out of there," David said.

"There has to be some way that they efficiently moved the water out of the tanks instead of by hand," Richard said.

"At least, we hope so," David agreed.

"I need to think for a minute," Richard said as he settled onto the ground and leaned back against the stone. He closed his eyes, tired from their journey yet excited that they were almost able to put their hands on an ancient treasure everyone believed to be lost.

"While you think, I'm going to see if I can find some lever system that operates this room."

David darted down the main aisle nearby and disappeared into the darkness.

Meanwhile, Richard climbed onto the ledge and circled the water. He stopped and stared out at the vast storage tanks. When he returned his attention to the one he was on, he noticed the water ripple slightly. He looked up to see a drainage pipe hovering overhead, not only near his position but over each tank.

That explains how they move the water.

"But why does this one look as if it was recently turned on?" Richard asked aloud.

As Richard was pondering this, more ripples spread across the water, this time from below as the level dropped rapidly. Just as the last portion disappeared down a drainage hole at the edge, David returned. He huffed as he leaned over the edge and inspected the now-empty tank.

"It worked," he said as a wide grin spread across his face.

"How did you do that?" Richard asked.

"I think the Moghuls were far more advanced than we know," David said. "There's a complex aquifer system in this fort."

"Where did the water go?" Richard asked.

"Beats me, and to be honest, I don't care. Let's get a move on."

Richard and David climbed inside the tank still damp in spots with small pools of standing water scattered across the bottom. They tackled the tedious job of searching for the hatch leading to where treasure could've been stored. Efficiently inspecting each possibility, they had covered about half the area before voices came from the entrance to the room. He noticed several flaming torches bobbing up and down in the distance.

"We've got company," Richard said.

They scrambled out and hid behind the wall of a nearby tank to assess the situation. Richard watched Vikrant lead three other men to number eighteen. With the exception of Vikrant, they all carried swords. Vikrant bounced around as he spoke quickly in Hindi. He waved his hands demonstratively as he appeared to explain how the special tank was identified.

"What do you want to do?" David asked.

"Are you suggesting that we just walk away and let this group of ragtag thieves plunder Man Singh's treasure?" Richard whispered.

"Why not? The point of our expedition is to ensure that the Germans don't get their hands on this, both for posterity's sake and to keep them from amassing such a fortune."

Richard scowled. "If we let these men take it, are we ensuring anything? Who's to say they wouldn't turn around and sell it to the Germans for next to nothing? And then what?"

"I think you're just itching for another fight."

Richard whipped his dagger out of his pocket. "I don't like this part of the job, but I've found it to be a necessary evil. And in this case, I don't see any other way."

David held his arm out, gesturing for Richard to proceed. Richard placed his index finger to his lips before he crept out into the open.

Sporting traditional Indian garb consisting of an *achkan* paired with a *sherwani*, the bandits were all peering over the edge into the empty tank when Richard eased up behind a man on the far end. David took a position behind a man on the opposite end from Richard and signaled with a nod. Both Army Intelligence agents grabbed the man in front of them and slammed his head against the stone. The thieves toppled to the ground, knocked out from the blunt hit. The result was a fight with even numbers.

Richard took on the other hulking man with a sword, while David squared off with Vikrant.

The sword-wielding thief took a big swipe at Richard, who drew back and narrowly avoided the blade. However, the attacker was off balance, allowing Richard the opportunity to strike. He slashed at the man's arm, forcing him to drop his sword as he clutched the wounded area.

Richard continued his assault by kicking the man in the face. He teetered for a moment and then collapsed.

Richard looked over in time to see David subdue Vikrant.

"Want to give me a hand over here?" David asked.

"It'll be my pleasure," Richard said. Using his *pagri's* ribbon, Richard tied up the attacker and then rushed over to David.

Richard snatched Vikrant's belt from around his waist and secured his hands behind him.

"Sorry about this, ole chap," David said as he slammed Vikrant's head against the side of the stone tank. Vikrant wilted after the blow and fell.

"Was that really necessary?" Richard asked. "I had a few more questions for him."

David patted down Vikrant and snatched the money from an inside jacket pocket. "There's a price to pay for double crossing us."

Richard and David scurried over to the other two men who were still out cold and also secured them using their belts.

"Now, let's get back to business," David said.

Richard and David climbed back inside the tank and resumed their inspection. After searching further for a few minutes, Richard squinted as he stared at one of the blocks. He reached outside and grabbed one of the torches that was still burning and held the flame close to the inscription etched onto the surface.

"Come take a look at this," Richard said.

David scrambled over to him and stared at the spot Richard lit. "What is that?"

"I don't know, but I don't see any markings like this on any of the other stones used to construct this tank."

Richard pulled out his dagger and started to scrape away

at the edges. When he was finished, he blew away the dust as a clearer marking came into focus.

"Let's try it," Richard said as he stood. He jammed his foot on top. Nothing happened.

"Move over," David said. "Let me give it a go."

David used the bottom of his heel and slammed it on the inscribed stone. Still no movement. David tried it again repeatedly, growling as he stomped. Richard watched intently and listened for any sign that a portal might be opening. But there wasn't any.

"Looks like it's back to the drawing board," Richard said.

Then before David could respond, the ground quivered as the sound of stone grinding against stone echoed in the cavernous room. Richard almost tripped as the bottom fanned downward into a spiral staircase. He jumped out of the way and waited for it to stop.

Without hesitating, Richard snatched up one of the torches and raced down the steps with David right behind. When they reached the foot of the stairs, they were inside a small chamber about ten feet square with an overhead clearance of about six feet. Richard had enough space to fit underneath without knocking his head against the ceiling, while David hunched over a bit to accommodate his larger frame.

Richard waved the torch around, methodically lighting each corner of the room. His eyes grew wide as he knelt down, collected a small jewel off the ground, and held the gem up before the flame.

"Would you look at that?" David asked. "A jewel."

"And the only one in here," Richard said. "Looks like the Reichswehr troops beat us to it."

CHAPTER 18

Dejected over losing the treasure, Richard sighed and kicked at the dusty floor. He sauntered up the steps in silence, unsure if he even wanted to discuss just how close they had been. After all the time and effort they had expended on preventing the Germans from getting the treasure, Richard grappled with the reality that he and David had failed.

They trudged out of the building in silence, leaving the men tied up. While exiting the room with all the storage tanks, Richard ignored the moans from Vikrant and the bandits and pressed forward.

David threw his arm around Richard's shoulder. "You learned a valuable lesson today: You can't win 'em all."

"That doesn't mean I can't be upset about not winning this one. We were so close. Not only do we have nothing to show for it now, but the Reichswehr has made off with all the treasure."

David shrugged. "Maybe, maybe not. We don't know if the treasure was removed last night or three hundred years ago or anywhere else in between."

"But based on the evidence I found with the water level and the signs that the tank was recently drained, it's pretty obvious that someone was just down there."

"They could've found the same thing we did. However, the good news is that if the Reichswehr stole away with the raja's fortune in the middle of the night after they tried to kill us, they wouldn't be able to get very far."

Richard cocked his head to one side and furrowed his brow. "Why's that?"

"The train out of Jaipur departs once at a day noon," David answered. "We've still got an hour to make the station and catch the Germans."

"And you don't think they would try to travel by some other method?"

"Not with the precious cargo they have."

Richard nodded. "Then we don't have any time to waste."

They hustled back toward the city and headed in the direction of the train depot. But they didn't get far before Richard noticed a truck puttering along the road loaded with a half dozen men. With the back of his hand, he hit David on the arm.

"Don't turn around now, but the Reichswehr unit is right behind," Richard said.

"If they get to the train station ahead of us, we might not be able to retrieve the treasure."

"Hold tight," Richard said. "I've got an idea."

A few meters ahead of them was a cow standing along the side of the road, free from being bothered in a culture that revered the animal. Richard glanced around to make sure no one was looking and gave the cow a shove in its rear end. Mildly annoyed, the animal looked back at Richard and remained pat.

The truck had picked up a little momentum as the street began to clear out of the vehicle's way—and Richard was running out of time. From a nearby street vendor, Richard snatched a carrot and held it in front of the cow before tossing the vegetable in the middle of the road. The bovine beast finally obliged, sauntering into the road to retrieve the prize. And then the cow didn't move, choosing to remain in its spot and enjoy its snack.

Richard scrambled aside and kept his head down, glancing up on occasion to see what course of action the Germans were taking. Wilhelm was riding in the front with the driver and reached over and sounded the horn, which earned him a sharp rebuke. Several of the men shouted at the animal, cursing in German and shaking their fists. But the cow still didn't budge.

As the local people milling around noticed the angry Reichswehr unit screaming at the sacred animal, they shouted at the Germans and shook their fists. Within a minute, an angry mob had assembled around the truck, drawing wide-eyed stares from the soldiers.

Richard seized the opportunity to make the problem a more permanent one for the Germans. Using the cover of the crowd, he crouched low and snaked beneath the truck, using his dagger to slash the two back tires. After finishing, he scrambled back out in time to avoid the tirade from the driver. The crowd started to disperse as he explained something to them and gestured with his hands for them to calm down.

Richard rejoined David as the two men ducked around the corner out of plain sight.

"Nice work," David said, nodding toward the chaotic scene. "I think they're going to be here for a while."

As the throng resumed daily tasks, several members of the Reichswehr unit became animated over the situation with the driver. He gestured for them to leave. And almost all of them did, while two of the soldiers remained behind with the truck and the driver, who called over a young boy before sending him off in a sprint.

"They've got the treasure," Richard said.

"What makes you think that?" David asked.

"Wilhelm stationed two men to guard the truck. Why would he do that if there wasn't anything valuable inside?"

"That's a good theory, and we need to test it."

"What do you propose?" Richard asked.

After developing a plan, five minutes later Richard emerged from around the corner and started waving his arms and shouting at the Germans. One of the men glared at Richard before leaping out of the back of the truck. Richard waited until the soldier edged closer before walking backward slowly. Once the man appeared engaged, Richard spun around and broke into a sprint. After about fifteen seconds, he glanced over his shoulder to see the German still in pursuit.

Richard veered toward the side of the road, pulling the Reichswehr operative farther away from the truck. Satisfied that the distance was sufficient, Richard raced across a bridge that spanned the Dravyavati River before jumping in once he reached the middle.

Richard plunged headlong into the cool water. When he resurfaced, he looked up and saw the German still standing on the bridge and watching carefully. Richard broke into a backstroke so he could keep an eye on the soldier. After a moment of swimming down the middle of the river, Richard veered toward the north bank. As he did, the operative raced across the bridge and down the near side.

However, Richard noticed the soldier's path and navigated toward the south bank. The German narrowed his eyes and shook his fist, yelling something that Richard couldn't understand. But he didn't need to since the man's face communicated exactly what he was thinking.

When Richard climbed out of the water, he hustled back to the spot where the truck had been stranded—but it was gone.

Everything was going just as he and David had planned.

CHAPTER 19

Wilhelm stared at his glass of ale, sneering at it as he rambled on about the poor quality of English beer in India. Seated next to him at the bar, Reinhard shrugged and sipped his water while keeping an eye on the rest of the Reichswehr unit. When Wilhelm finished his rant, he glanced at his watch.

"Did our driver say when he would have the tires changed?" Wilhelm asked. "The train is scheduled to leave in half an hour."

"He said it wouldn't take more than fifteen or twenty minutes," Reinhard said. "He should walk through those doors any minute now."

"Any extra minute is a minute too long," Wilhelm said as he studied his glass and turned up his nose. "The English never understood how to brew good weissbier, and now I have to drink *this*."

"You can choose something else, sir."

"You're right," Wilhelm said as he seized his glass and held it up in the air. He proceeded to pour the entire contents onto the floor. "I think I'll have a different drink," he said to the bartender.

The bartender glared at Wilhelm, apparently unpleased by his blatant show of disrespect.

"And I'd like something now," Wilhelm said.

"What would you like, *sir*?" the bartender asked as he narrowed his eyes.

Wilhelm didn't answer. He was distracted by a troop member who stormed into the pub, shouting excitedly.

"Slow down," Reinhard said.

But the man continued, waving his arms expressively. "The truck is gone."

Wilhelm stood. "Weren't you supposed to be watching it?"

At this point, several of the other German soldiers joined the discussion at the bar. Wilhelm pursed his lips and subtly shook his head, clenching his fist and his teeth. And when the soldier didn't respond quickly enough, Wilhelm grabbed the man by his shoulders and shook him.

"I asked you a question. Weren't you supposed to be watching our belongings?"

The man nodded, quaking as he didn't elaborate.

"Well, tell me what happened," Wilhelm demanded. "And you better have a good excuse."

"It was Richard Halliburton, sir. We saw him. He was taunting us. Jans remained behind while I went after him."

"And where's Jans?"

"He was unconscious and lying along the side of the road with his hands tied behind his back."

Wilhelm took a deep breath and exhaled slowly. "He's not working alone. I don't care if you have to tear this city apart. Find Halliburton and his accomplice."

Wilhelm watched his men scatter before he turned to Reinhard.

"Sir," Reinhard began, "we're going to need some help to find them."

Wilhelm shrugged. "They will stick out here. It shouldn't

be that difficult to find them in Jaipur, especially if we incentivize the people."

"They're not going to parade themselves down the middle of the street. It's going to take a more concerted effort if you intend to bring them into the open. We must lure them out."

"What bait do we possibly have?" Wilhelm asked as he threw his head back and looked up at the ceiling. "We need help from above."

"Or help from the British," said a man next to Wilhelm.

He spun on his barstool to see Felix Ludwig standing next to him along with Maredumilli magistrate Alex Fullerton.

"If you hadn't botched your assignment, we wouldn't even be in this mess," Wilhelm said with a sneer before returning to his drink.

Ludwig put his hands up. "Sir, I would appreciate the opportunity to explain. I—"

"I don't want to hear your excuses," Wilhelm said, waving dismissively. "They're tiresome and will only underscore your inability to finish the job I asked you to do."

Ludwig shifted his weight from one foot to the other. "In that case, let me make it up to you by helping you catch these two agents. They're quite adept at disrupting our plans."

"And what makes you think you can do that?"

"Perhaps my confidence is my greatest weakness at times, but I know we can flush them out with the help of the local police."

"And then what?" Wilhelm asked. "We're just going to let some inept constables handle the miscreants?"

Ludwig shook his head. "We only need the police to force the men out into the open. Then we capture them ourselves and handle the situation privately."

"And what makes you think they'll go for that?"

"This man right here," Ludwig said, slapping Fullerton on the back. "Want a drink?"

Fullerton shook his head and slumped into a chair at a nearby table.

"He's not very pleased about being here, but he left me no choice after his faulty prison security cost us a chance to eliminate Mr. Halliburton and his associate," Ludwig said.

Wilhelm's eyebrows shot upward. "How are you going to make this right, Felix?"

Ludwig rubbed his hands together as a wry smile leaked across his face. "Mr. Fullerton is going to make it right by alerting law enforcement here in Jaipur that two Americans stole treasure belonging to India and intend to smuggle it out of the city. Isn't that right, Mr. Fullerton?"

"This wasn't exactly part of our deal," he said as he turned toward Wilhelm. "I only agreed to assure safe passage through the country, not enlist the queen's resources to help you catch someone who has taken a treasure from you that was stolen from a castle here."

"Our agreement has changed," Wilhelm said. "Now go make it happen. And don't even think about showing your face to me again until after you've implored every soldier in Jaipur to find Halliburton and his associate."

Wilhelm buried his head in his hands and closed his eyes. Richard Halliburton had become a veritable thorn in Wilhelm's side, and he was growing more irritated by the moment. The operation in Jaipur should have been a smooth one but was quickly turning into Luxor all over again.

"We'll figure this out, sir," Reinhard said.

"This problem should've been solved long ago at sea, but apparently some of my *wolfsrudel* aren't as skilled as they need to be."

Wilhelm spun on his stool and turned to find a man standing a few feet away.

"Sir, are you Karl Wilhelm?" he asked.

"Who's asking?" Wilhelm grumbled

"I have a telegram for you, sir."

Wilhelm snatched the envelope from the man's hand and read it silently.

"What is it?" Reinhard asked.

"It's a note from General Seeckt," Wilhelm said sliding it to Reinhard. "Read it yourself."

Reinhard took the note and read it aloud: "Send progress report on operation. The council is growing impatient. Results required."

"You understand what this means, don't you?" Wilhelm asked.

Reinhard nodded. "He's going to replace us if we don't bring back the treasure."

"Or worse."

"Worse?" Reinhard asked as he cocked his head to the side.

"If I know General Seeckt like I think I do, he'll send a team to eliminate us first. We know too much for him to risk letting us return to other positions. If we don't get our hands on this treasure, Richard Halliburton will be the least of our worries."

CHAPTER 20

RICHARD TURNED OFF THE MAIN STREET AND HUSTLED down an alley, dodging merchants carting their wares on top of their heads and small children scurrying behind their parents. His clothes were still wet but drying off quickly in the sweltering heat. Not that Richard minded. His plan to draw away the guards had worked to perfection while David had managed to subdue the other Reichswehr agent and escape with the truck. The difficult part was over. All they had to do was get out of the city without the Reichswehr seeing them.

After a couple minutes, Richard reached the rendezvous point, the back corner of an open market about a half-mile from Jaipur's busiest thoroughfare. He scanned the area for David and didn't immediately see him. However, Richard heard someone calling for him in a whisper from behind. He spun around to find David with his head poking through a pair of drawn curtains.

"Psst. Richard, over here," David said.

Richard darted into the small opening in the curtain and joined David.

"Do you have the truck?" Richard asked.

"And the treasure," David said. "But we need to get out of here fast before anyone gets wind of what's going on."

"Didn't you pay off the driver?"

David nodded. "I did, but that's not going to matter once the Reichswehr unit starts offering large sums of money to whoever will give us up."

"Why don't we just drive to the train station?"

"We'll never make it," David said. "It leaves in five minutes, and it would take at least ten just to get there. By then it would be too late."

Richard shrugged. "So we sit and wait it out. It shouldn't be that difficult."

"The Reichswehr troops will be hovering around the station just waiting for us to try and board. I would say we could head a few miles out of town and try to make a run for it to get on the train, but we'd never make it."

"Why's that?"

"You need to see this treasure."

David poked his head outside the curtains again to see if anyone was watching them. When he deemed the area clear, he led Richard back to a home a couple blocks away. They cut down an alley and entered through a side door.

"The storage door opens to the back, which is how Sandeep gets his truck in and out of here."

"Sandeep. Is that the driver?"

"The one and only. And he's quite the character."

David knocked on the door. Sandeep opened it slightly before recognizing his high-paying guest, waving him inside.

"Who's this?" Sandeep pointed his dagger at Richard.

"He's my colleague, Richard. Richard, Sandeep. Sandeep, Richard. Now that we're all acquainted, let's get back to planning how we're going to get out of here with the treasure."

Richard shook hands with Sandeep, who then sheathed his blade and spun around. He strode to the corner of the room, picked up a pungi, and then began playing it.

"What's that all about?" Richard asked, gesturing toward Sandeep.

"Truck for hire by day, snake charmer by night," David said.

Richard watched as Sandeep removed the lid from a basket and a cobra's head slowly rose above the rim. The animal shifted from side to side, appearing to follow the end of Sandeep's *pungi.*

"I'm not sure how I feel about holing up in a place with a venomous snake," Richard said. "You know I'm all for adventure and I love animals, but this is pushing the limits, even for me."

"Oh, I'm sure the snake his harmless," David said, waving dismissively.

At that moment, the cobra hissed and struck at Sandeep.

"Harmless? You think that's harmless? It's a snake, David. It's poisonous enough to put down an elephant."

"Not when they're hypnotized."

"They're not hypnotized. They're just following that instrument around. And there's no absolutely no way I want to stay in here."

David huffed a laugh through his nose. "Don't go all soft on me now."

A knock at the door ended the conversation, and Sandeep covered the basket and shuffled across the room. He peeked outside before allowing another man inside.

The man's brow was furrowed and he spoke rapidly in Hindi, waving his arms about.

"What's going on?" David asked when the man finished.

Sandeep sighed and shook his head. "This is my cousin, Rajiv. He said the British constables are everywhere in the market. Someone has notified them that a major Indian artifact was stolen from the Jaigahr Fort today. And the description matches the two of you."

"That's absurd," Richard said. "We didn't . . ."

Richard stopped and buried his head in his hands. With someone within the British government on the side of the Reichswehr unit, he realized the fight was an unfair one.

"We should call Harvey and see if he can straighten this thing out for us," Richard said.

"Absolutely not," David said. "He won't like getting dragged into what's likely to be a diplomatic mess, not to mention a cultural one. Plus, our cover will be blown. None of those outcomes seem preferable to me."

"Aren't they preferable to the Reichswehr sneaking out of India with millions of dollars in stolen treasure?"

David shrugged. "Perhaps, but we don't get to make that call. If we're going to resolve this situation, we're going to have to handle it some other way."

Sandeep nodded. "And you're going to need a very good disguise if you intend to go anywhere in the city."

Rajiv started talking again, lines creasing in his forehead as he spoke.

"What did Rajiv say?" David asked.

"He said there's also a bounty out for the two of you," Sandeep replied. "It won't be long before anyone who thinks they saw you enter this place with me will be reporting it to the British authorities in hopes of receiving a nice sum of money."

"I'm sure you can convince them otherwise," David said as he dangled another ten-pound note in front of Sandeep.

He snatched the money and pocketed it. "I will do my best, but I can't promise how long you have before the British charge in here. And I prefer not to get entangled in this affair."

"You want us out of here?" Richard asked, cutting his eyes over at the snake basket.

"I would greatly appreciate it if you were gone by the morning," Sandeep said. "It's nothing personal. I'm sure you understand."

David and Richard both nodded.

"Looks like we've waded into waist-deep trouble here," David said. "This won't have an easy solution."

Richard took a deep breath and then exhaled slowly. "Actually, I think there's a way we could wriggle out of this and still reach our goals, which is preventing the Germans from getting the treasure and evading a situation that could cause a diplomatic nightmare for Harvey and the American government."

"I'm listening," David said.

"It's really quite simple, to be honest."

"Well, stop dancing around and say your idea, Richard. You're driving me nuts."

Richard grinned. "We're going to hide the treasure back in the fort."

David grimaced. "You might want to take a look at the treasure first."

CHAPTER 21

Richard followed David into the back of the truck, which was covered with white linen. Grabbing a crowbar lying in the bed, David pried open one of the crates. Inside was a wooden chest piled high with jewels and gold. Richard plunged his fingers into the treasures as they spilled out over the top and splashed into the bed of the truck. Staring wide-eyed at the haul, Richard's mouth fell agape.

"There's four more just like this one," David said.

"How much do you think this is worth?" Richard asked.

David shrugged. "Millions and millions. If this isn't enough to get the German military back up and running to full strength, it'd go a long way toward accomplishing that."

"I've never seen anything like this."

"I doubt that Reichswehr unit had either," David said. "It's why they enlisted the help of the British. The Germans are going to claim they discovered this, pay off the Brits and Indian officials with a portion of the spoils, and disappear back to Deutschland."

"We can't let that happen."

"You've got that right," David said as he nodded. "But this does present a serious obstacle to what you just suggested. How do you propose we sneak all of this treasure back into the fort to hide it? We can't very well wheel it up there in carts in broad daylight."

Richard and David exited the truck and drew a cord, pulling the covering taut so no one could see inside.

"Did Sandeep look back here?" Richard whispered.

David shook his head. "I told him that it was just some artifacts the Germans were stealing which need to be returned to their home."

"If he sees this, he's going to get greedy and jeopardize everything."

"Just leave that to me," David said. "So far, so good when it comes to satisfying Sandeep."

A shrill noise from the corner of the room arrested Richard's attention. He glanced toward the sound and saw Rajiv playing with a monkey, which had climbed up Rajiv's back and was covering his eyes.

Wide-eyed, Richard glanced at David. "These are the people who are going to help us get out of this situation? Snake charming, a monkey—it's like we've fallen into the middle of a carnival act."

"Isn't the carnival where you would go if you wanted to disappear?" David asked with a shrug. "Besides, it's not like I handpicked these guys from hundreds of job applicants. Sandeep was driving the truck, and Rajiv is part of the package."

"How did we get the short end of the stick here?"

"The what?" David asked with a furrowed brow.

"It's what we say in Memphis when you get a bad deal."

"We can't do anything about how we got here, but we can change our future. Now, let's figure out a way to get this treasure back to the fort and get the hell out of here."

David looked down at his leg as something tugged on his pants. Wearing a toothy grin, the monkey looked up at David and squawked again.

David knelt and held his hand out to the monkey, which circled him several times before running back to Rajiv. As David eased to his feet, he patted his back pocket. He put his hands on his hips and smiled.

"That's quite an animal you have there," he said to Rajiv.

Rajiv nodded and smiled.

"His English isn't that great," Sandeep said. "Let me translate."

Sandeep relayed what David had said before softly answering, "Thank you."

"And I believe it stole my wallet," David said.

Rajiv's forehead creased as he turned to Sandeep for translation. Sandeep glared at Rajiv and spoke sternly to him in a hushed tone.

"My cousin apologizes," Sandeep said. "I've warned him before that not everyone thinks that joke is funny."

"But it isn't a joke, is it?" David replied. "How often does he pull that trick on unsuspecting people milling around the market?"

Sandeep strode across the room with his hands in the air. "Rajiv didn't mean to offend you. He was only playing around with Smita."

"Smita?" Richard asked.

"It's the name of the monkey," Sandeep said. "It means 'happy face'."

"There's never been a more appropriate name," Richard said. "That monkey knows how to smile."

"And how to pick my pocket," David said.

"I apologize on Rajiv's behalf," Sandeep said. "I'll make sure he instructs Smita not to do it again."

Richard sighed. "Look, I really need to get a better idea of where we are so I can figure out how we're going to get out of here."

"You can get to the roof by using those stairs in the corner," Sandeep said.

Richard nodded and gestured for David to join him. The pair hustled up two flights of stairs before emerging into the day's fading sunlight atop the building. In the distance, Richard saw Fort Jaigahr's walls rising above the ridge that surrounded the city. Though it was getting late, people were still trudging up the long ramp to the gate entrance, hoping to take a quick look around at the majestic and ancient structure before the sun set. And while some people slogged their way up the steep hill to access the fort, the smarter and wealthier patrons rode on the backs of elephants.

"What are you thinking?" David asked after a few minutes.

"I'm thinking it's nearly impossible to figure out a way into that fort, especially with all the British constables buzzing about like Tennessee gnats. They'd catch us for sure if we went a more conventional way."

"Maybe we need to rethink our strategy," David said.

"No, our strategy is solid," Richard said. "However, our methods need to be tested for me to feel confident about pulling off a job of this magnitude."

"We may not have much of a choice about anything," David said as he nodded toward a corner a few blocks away where teams of constables worked their way along the street.

"Think they know we're staying with Sandeep?" Richard asked.

"Let's not wait around to find out."

They raced back down the steps and rushed inside the storage room where Sandeep had parked the truck. He shot a look at them as his eyes grew wide.

"What is it?" Sandeep asked.

"The police are coming this way," David said. "We need to hide the artifacts now."

"I can help," Sandeep offered.

David shook his head. "You and Rajik go inside. It's better that we hide it in case you get questioned. If you know nothing, you won't look guilty when they start demanding answers."

"What do I tell them?" Sandeep asked.

"Tell them that you had two flat tires and the Germans who hired you took all their belongings out of the truck and hired another one that drove by so you could go find help," David said.

"But what if they don't believe me?"

"If you can charm a snake, I have full confidence you can convince the police you are innocent," David said. "We'll make it worth all this trouble, I promise."

Sandeep sighed and waved Rajik over to him along with Smita. They exited the room and entered the house.

"You think we have time to hide all this treasure?" Richard asked.

"There's only one way to find out."

David found some space in the corner, which was room enough for all the chests, while Richard found a large burlap blanket that could be used to cover the entire fortune—and themselves if necessary.

They worked quickly, unloading each ancient chest and setting it down in the designated spot. After three minutes, they'd managed to unload everything and spread the blanket over it. They inspected the back of the truck to make sure no stray jewels or gold pieces had fallen out before heading toward the entryway that led back into the house.

Richard crouched low and placed his ear against the door.

"Do you hear anything?" David asked.

"Yeah, they're coming this way."

Richard and David scrambled toward the corner in search

of a place to hide. Unable to fit comfortably in the space with the treasure, Richard located a pair of hand-woven baskets in the far corner, large enough for them to hide in.

"Make sure there aren't any snakes in yours," David said with a wry smile.

"That's not funny," Richard said as he poked his head inside. Satisfied that the basket was snake free, he jumped in and pulled the top down tight.

Richard listened as Sandeep led the officers on a tour around the room.

"Here's the truck," Sandeep said. "Feel free to check the back. I don't even know what they placed inside. They just asked me for a ride to the train station. And while we were on our way, I stopped for a cow in the road. When the road was clear, I realized I had two flat tires and couldn't go anywhere."

"And then what happened?" asked an officer.

"These men took their stuff and left, so I came back to my house."

"He's lying," said a man in a German accent.

Richard peered through a slit in the basket and noticed one of the men with the officers was a member of Wilhelm's team.

"Who's truck is this?" asked the officer.

"It's mine," Sandeep said. "My uncle died last year and left it for me to carry on the family business. It's what I do to take care of my aunt."

"Where is the artifact?" the German demanded. "I know you have it hidden here somewhere."

"Look around for yourself," Sandeep said. "I didn't take anything."

The officer scanned the truck again before shrugging and turning to the German. "It looks clear to me. He seems like he's telling the truth."

"He's full of lies," the German roared before lunging toward Sandeep. One of the other officers held back the Reichswehr operative as Sandeep jumped back to avoid contact.

The constable started to poke around, peeking inside boxes and baskets lying about. He had worked half the room before another officer raced in to join them.

"Sir, we've got a situation that requires your immediate attention," he said.

"I'm in the middle of an investigation here," the officer replied.

"It can't wait. There's an altercation at the market, and it's growing."

"In that case, I think we're done here—for now," the constable said. "Thank you for your time."

The officers forced the German outside through a side door and into the alley.

Richard waited for several minutes before climbing out of the basket. David followed him, moaning as he stretched.

"What was in the truck?" Sandeep asked.

"Don't worry," David said. "You did a great job of staying calm. I don't think they suspect you."

"But that German soldier is crazy. What is he doing here anywhere? What are they looking for?" Sandeep asked.

Smita scurried around at their feet, screeching and dancing with a grin on his face.

"You won't have to concern yourself with this after tonight," Richard said. "We're going to get everything out of here."

"How do you propose to do that?" David asked.

Richard knelt down and offered his arm to Smita. The monkey scrambled up and then perched on Richard's shoulder.

"I've got a plan," Richard said with a wink. "Now go up on the roof and make sure those officers aren't coming back."

CHAPTER 22

Wilhelm glared at Alex Fullerton upon receiving the news that the British officers hadn't arrested the truck driver who disappeared with the Reichswehr unit's discovery. After pacing around the room several times, Wilhelm stopped and jabbed his finger into Fullerton's chest.

"You're supposed to make sure that the police are assisting us," Wilhelm said. "It seems they aren't as interested in helping us out despite your conversation."

Fullerton took a step back and raised his hands in air. "I can't make the authorities apprehend those two. I can only share what they've been accused of and what they did in my district."

Wilhelm's nostrils flared as he held a steady gaze on Fullerton. "The reason we're paying you is to ensure that our expedition across India runs smoothly. Instead, you failed to keep those two miscreants in prison and now they're here—and they're ruining all our plans."

"I'm sorry for the inconvenience," Fullerton said. "Things here aren't like they are in Germany. We can't just go around flinging people into jail on a whim."

"Felix told me you found a way to do that in Maredumilli. So, why not here?"

"This isn't my city."

"Then make it yours," Wilhelm said.

"I've done all I can do for now."

"Go put pressure on the chief superintendent. I'm holding you accountable if this situation isn't resolved to my satisfaction."

"But, sir, you must understand, I—"

Wilhelm pointed at the door. "Go."

Reinhard, who had been out with the other troops scouring the streets for any signs of Richard Halliburton and his accomplice, entered the room as Fullerton was exiting. He didn't attempt to step aside, putting the full weight of his shoulder into Reinhard.

Reinhard stopped and stared at Fullerton, but the man didn't turn around as he stormed out of the room.

"What did you say to him?" Reinhard asked, nodding in the direction of Fullerton.

Before Wilhelm could answer, the sound of the front door slamming echoed through the room.

"Some men need extra motivation to do the job they're required to do," Wilhelm said while staring into his glass of port. "Especially that man."

"I take it the police haven't found our two meddlers," Reinhard said, settling down onto the stool next to Wilhelm.

"They found the truck, but it was empty," Wilhelm said. "The driver said that we cleaned out all our belongings so he drove home on two flat tires so he could fix them there."

"And we're just letting him walk away?" Reinhard asked.

"It was a sensitive situation, but we will pay him a visit tonight now that we know where he lives."

"You think that will make a difference? If he believes we took the treasures, then—"

Wilhelm shook his head, sneering in disgust as he

interrupted. "He knows exactly what he's doing. I have no doubt that Mr. Halliburton is paying the driver handsomely to keep quiet or has cut him in on the spoils. Either way, we will have a tough time convincing him to join us without sufficient motivation."

Reinhard sighed and ordered a drink. "Sometimes, there are people who will never be swayed to our way of thinking. You can't reason with them. In many cases, they're unable to see how they're wrong. So you have to take a different approach when forced coercion won't bring about what you desire."

"Is there a point to your philosophizing?"

"I'm getting there," Reinhard said. "When I was in school, there was a boy in my class who had a toy sailboat. He carried it everywhere he went like it was a pet but never once placed with it in the pond on the school grounds. One day, I asked if I could play with his boat. He refused and retreated from the rest of the class. I decided to ask every day because I wanted him to see what an incredible toy it was and how it could float on the water. As I pressed him, he became angrier and more violent. One day, I attempted to take it, but he flew at me, knocking me to the ground. We fought for a few minutes until one of the teachers saw us and tore us apart. I received a warning for the incident and was told that if I engaged another student like that again, I would be expelled. That wasn't an option since I was terrified of my father and what he might do to me. So, I decided that if I was going to get my hands on that boat, I needed another strategy. The next day, I spoke with all the boys in my class and offered them a small bounty to retrieve the toy boat. And it worked. The boy just handed it over to another student, who promptly brought it to me. I raced to the water and launched the boat, much to the excitement of everyone—

except the little boy, of course."

"I almost shed a tear," Wilhelm said, his response dripping with sarcasm.

"Look, we're in foreign territory and not in a position to impose our will on that truck driver. But we might be able to accomplish the same goal by making it worth the while of other people in the city to help us out."

"We've already placed a bounty on him."

Reinhard nodded. "So we increase it. Someone will come forward if the reward is handsome enough."

"What amount do you think will coax the people of Jaipur to take action? A hundred pounds?"

"Two hundred," Reinhard said. "They'll never get out of here alive."

"Make it so, "Wilhelm said.

Reinhard sprang from his seat and then exited the pub. Wilhelm ordered another drink.

* * *

RAJIV WAS RELAXING ON THE ROOFTOP, SMOKING HIS PIPE AS his after dinner treat. He was exhausted from a hard day of work and settled into his favorite chair to watch the sun slip beneath the horizon. The sounds of music filled the streets as it did every evening in Jaipur, while Rajiv rocked gently to the rhythms of the festive songs.

Most evenings, Rajiv shared the moment with Smita. But not tonight. Rajiv's monkey had taken a liking to the Americans and had become their shadow. No amount of enticement could draw Smita away from his new friends, who didn't seem bothered by the animal's mischievous spirit. But Smita knew his way home, and if he was being ignored, he'd either split or let everyone know about it.

Rajiv was halfway through his smoke when he noticed a big commotion in the street. He got out of his chair and strode to the edge of the roof so he could see what was happening. Men raced down the street, shouting at people sitting outside on their doorsteps. Meanwhile, other groups of boys huddled up before dispersing in opposite directions.

"Rajiv!" a young man from the street called out.

"What's happening?" Rajiv asked with a smile.

"There are two American criminals on the loose in Jaipur."

"What have they done?"

The young man shrugged. "I don't know. But what I do know is that a constable told me there is a reward of two hundred pounds to anyone who knows where they are."

"Two hundred pounds?" Rajiv asked as his mouth fell agape.

"That's right. You heard me correctly. Two hundred pounds."

Rajiv spun around and dropped his pipe on the table next to his chair. He raced back inside and didn't stop running.

Sandeep needs to know about this—or maybe he doesn't.

CHAPTER 23

RICHARD AND DAVID WRAPPED THEIR HEADS WITH navy-blue cloths to form neatly tied *pagris* and donned matching white shirts and *dhotis* before venturing out into the streets. Smita followed after them before he latched onto Richard's leg and summited him, perching on his shoulder.

"You're quite persistent," Richard said to Smita, who only responded with a toothy grin. "And cheeky too."

They shuffled along, keeping their heads down as they walked toward the fort.

"You realize this mission is doomed," David said. "Once this fails, we're going to—"

"I'm going to sock you in the mouth if you continue to spew such nonsense," Richard said. "This plan is going to work."

David ignored the threat. "As I was saying, when this plan doesn't work, we're going to need to be proactive in contacting Harvey so he can get another team of agents in place to prevent the Reichswehr from stealing out of the country with an immense fortune."

"There's only one problem to your depressing scenario," Richard said.

"What's that?"

"We still have the entire fortune. The Germans aren't going to get their hands on it; we're going to see to that."

"I think we'd be better off trying to sneak it onto a train and take it away from Jaipur," David suggested. "We'd at least have somewhat better odds."

"Nonsense," Richard said. "We need to do the thing they'd least expect. For all we know, they think we're trying to steal the treasure away for our country. Returning it to the fort is not what they'll expect. And if we do that, we can get out of here without any further charges being brought against us."

"I heard that little phrase—further charges," David said. "That's because you know there are already charges pending against us."

"Yes, but we're in a larger city now. We can get those reduced or dropped without having to return to the dark forest to reclaim our good names."

"The British legal system doesn't work like ours," David warned. "Getting a fair trial isn't a given."

"It's not a given back home either, but at least it's more likely than not."

"I wouldn't be so sure about that."

Richard sighed. "Well, all this yammering on about nothing is worthless because this plan is going to work. You'll see. Isn't that right, Smita?"

The monkey clapped his hands and grinned.

"When you can only get an animal to agree with you, you should know that something is amiss," David said.

"You can thank me later," Richard said. "In the meantime, I'm going to pretend like you didn't just doubt me."

"Sorry, it's in my nature," David said. "I'm just not as confident as you are."

Fifteen minutes later, they arrived near the outskirts of Jaipur where several tourist camps were stacked next to each other, all of them with some gimmicky mechanism for transporting sightseers up the long ramp leading to Fort Jaigahr. For the purposes of Richard's plan, Thomas Cook & Son's tour company appeared to be the most promising and also the most challenging. It utilized a fleet of elephants to usher customers up and down the pathway that zigged and zagged to the fort's gate, a much more exotic method compared to horses or the traditional rickshaws.

With only an hour of daylight left and access to the fort closed more than an hour earlier, the stables holding the elephants were locked. Richard shook the gates just to be sure, and they didn't open.

"Now what?" David asked.

"We need to get inside if we're going to pull this off tonight."

Richard knelt and peered toward the far wall where a rack of keys was affixed. He helped Smita down to the ground.

"You're gonna get the monkey to do this?" David asked before sighing. "I hope you're beginning to see that my skepticism is appropriate."

Richard ignored David and gestured toward the keys. "Go get them for me, Smita. Be a good boy."

Smita eased through the bars and bounded toward the area where Richard pointed. Looking back once more, the monkey received the affirmation he needed and leaped up the wall. He grabbed one of the empty nodules with one hand and swung up to snatch a set of keys with the other. Once he hit the ground, he scurried to Richard.

"Good boy," Richard said, rubbing the monkey's head.

Richard stood and cast a sideways glance at David. "You were saying?"

"Dumb luck," David said as he cracked a smile.

Richard opened the gate, and then they slipped inside to inspect the elephants. Several of the elephants were lying down, their decorative crimson saddle blankets hung up in the corner of each stall. He climbed over one of the fences to inspect it more closely.

"What do you think?" David asked. "Is this going to work?"

Richard shoved his hand inside and felt along the stitching. The strength of the fabric and the depth of the pockets were the two major determining factors. Satisfied that they would get the job done, he turned toward David.

"We have a winner," Richard said. "This is going to work."

"We need to get back before it gets too late, especially if we intend on transporting all of the treasure back here tonight," David said.

"Before we do that, we need to go see Sandeep again."

"What for? Those Reichswehr operatives might be waiting for us there."

"We need his help," Richard said.

"It also jeopardizes the entire mission if one of the constables wants to question him again."

"They're done with him. The Germans are going to focus their search for us. And as long as we keep our heads down—"

"We're going to look rather suspicious, with or without Sandeep."

Richard smiled and slapped David on the back. "Trust me. We'll be fine."

They hustled toward the center of the city, which had become much more lively as the sun was getting closer to disappearing for the day. Richard and David kept their heads down as they wove in and out of the people bustling through the streets.

When they drew near to Sandeep's house, they darted down an alley, approaching from behind.

"If you're so sure no one is going to be there, why aren't we marching up to the front door?" David asked.

"We should still be cautious," Richard said as Smita squawked. "See, even Smita agrees."

"Just keep Smita quiet," David said. "And just for the record, I think this is a bad idea."

"Your dissent has been registered."

Richard headed up a stairwell that led to the rooftop. However, just as he ascended high enough to see the balcony, he stopped and eased back down.

"What is it?" whispered David.

"Wilhelm is here with several of his men," Richard said. "They're speaking with Sandeep."

"I knew it," David said. "He's turning us in."

Smita sprang off Richard's shoulder and raced onto the balcony.

Richard and David quietly descended the steps, listening to Wilhelm's conversation with Sandeep.

"There's a handsome reward if you have any information about where these men are," Wilhelm said.

"How much again?" Sandeep asked.

"Two hundred pounds," Wilhelm said.

"Well, in that case—"

Smita disrupted their conversation by screeching.

"What is it?" Sandeep asked.

Richard hit the last step when he could almost feel everyone looking at him. The scuffle of feet toward the edge made him turn around for a quick glance. They were all standing near the stairs and staring at him.

"There he is," Wilhelm said. "Seize him."

Richard and David broke into a dead sprint.

CHAPTER 24

Wilhelm shouted orders to the Reichswehr agents hustling down the steps in pursuit the two U.S. Army Intelligence operatives. Perched above the city on the second story roof of Sandeep's house, Wilhelm held a powerful vantage point and used his booming voice to keep the hunt close. He watched as Richard and David wove back and forth like a pair of rats in a maze. However, after a couple minutes, Wilhelm could no longer see them or his men.

"Let's go," he said to Reinhard.

"What if they come back?" Reinhard asked.

"Give them more credit than that. They didn't get this far by making dumb decisions. Now, come on."

Wilhelm reached inside his jacket and fingered his gun. He drew it out, keeping it aimed toward the ground.

"Put that away," Reinhard said in a stern tone. "We're archeologists, not soldiers. Remember?"

Wilhelm didn't allow anyone to speak to him so harshly, except for Reinhard. The unit's second in command took advantage of the permission granted to him to state serious concerns frankly when necessary. Wilhelm never liked it when Reinhard talked to him in such a manner, though there was no protest.

Wilhelm shoved his gun back into its holster as they navigated through the alleyways of the city.

"Where did you last see them?" Reinhard asked.

"They were about three blocks to the east from where we were."

"And did you notice any pattern to their escape?"

"No, it was sheer chaos, a race for survival."

"Don't worry, sir. We're going to find them—and the treasure."

"We better," growled Wilhelm.

As they approached an intersection, they cut to the right and dodged the onslaught of people shuffling home as nightfall had set in and the evening revelry in the streets was dying down. After a matter of minutes, Wilhelm realized he hadn't seen a single member of his crew.

"Where did they go?" Wilhelm said. "They couldn't just disappear like that, at least not two Americans in the middle of an Indian city."

"But there are quite a number of British people in this area, so it might be easier to blend in than you think," Reinhard said.

"It's either that or we're stupid," Wilhelm said. "They could still be right here, just beneath our noses."

"Don't beat yourself up over this, sir. We were at a significant disadvantage from the beginning. They only have to avoid capture, while we have to pluck them from an eclectic mixture of people in Jaipur. I don't need to tell you that our task is far more challenging."

Wilhelm growled. He needed to take his aggression out on someone, and he preferred it to be the two Americans. However, he wasn't sure that was going to happen any time soon.

A man pushed his way past the German commander and

his second and drove his shoulder into Wilhelm.

"Hey! Watch it," Wilhelm sneered.

The man didn't flinch, continuing his route as if nothing of significance had happened.

"Hey! I'm talking to you," Wilhelm barked again.

Unresponsive to Wilhelm's angry calls, the man continued trudging along. And Wilhelm decided to make an example out of the man. Without hesitating, Wilhelm rushed up grabbed the man by his collar, pulling him backward. Wilhelm drew back his clenched fist and prepared to strike when Reinhard put his hand on Wilhelm's shoulder.

"Not now," Reinhard said. "The last thing you need to do is make a scene. Just let him go."

Wilhelm released the man with a slight shove and stormed off, resuming his search for the Americans. As Wilhelm navigated through the tight quarters of Jaipur's alleys, a Reichswehr agent gasped for air as he approached the unit's leader.

"What is it?" Wilhelm asked.

"They're gone, sir. They just vanished into thin air," the soldier said.

"That's not what I wanted to hear," Wilhelm said.

"I know, sir, but they obviously know their way around this area, because they were right in front of us and then disappeared without a trace. We searched everywhere."

Another soldier hustled over to Reinhard and whispered in his ear.

Reinhard put his hand on Wilhelm's back. "Sir, let's forget about Halliburton for now. At least we have the treasure back."

"Someone found it?" Wilhelm asked.

Reinhard nodded. "One of our men located the crates tucked away in the back corner of a storage room downstairs where the truck was located."

"I'm still upset about losing those American agents, but this treasure is what we really came for. Lead the way. I want to verify this for myself."

"Of course," Reinhard said. "That's understandable. Follow me."

Wilhelm shoved his hands into his pockets and fingered the letter for Reinhard. If anyone deserved to know the truth about what was going on back home, Reinhard did—and he'd soon be able to get back to his family once the Reichswehr unit transported all the treasure to Germany. And even though Wilhelm felt like he was never going to get a more opportune time to share the news, he hesitated. He needed to keep Reinhard focused until they could get the vast fortune out of India without further incident.

Upon return to Sandeep's house, Wilhelm fought his way to the front of the pack and charged inside. He ordered his men to open one of the crates so he could verify the contents and proceed with making plans to transport the treasure.

"Come on," Wilhelm said to the two soldiers working on opening the crate. "You need to work faster. We don't have much time left if this is what I think it is."

One of the soldiers wedged the bent claw into a tight space between the lid and the top of the box. With a snap of his wrists, the bar ripped nails out of the top and sprang it open.

Wilhelm leaned over the edge and peered inside, his eyes widening as he stared into the crate.

CHAPTER 25

RICHARD SCANNED THE AREA THROUGH HIS BINOCULARS. After a moment, he returned his focus to the Sandeep's house, just outside the small courtyard leading to the back where he'd parked his truck. Sandeep and Rajiv watched quietly as Wilhelm paced around with a scowl on his face.

"What's going on?" David asked.

"Wilhelm is irritated about something," Richard said, as he handed the binoculars to David. "See for yourself."

After a few seconds, David nodded as he continued to watch. "Something's got him riled up, that's for sure."

"What's he doing now?" Richard asked.

David cursed under his breath. "They found the crates, and they're about to open them."

"And?"

"One of Wilhelm's goons is prying one open right now." A pause. "They're looking inside and . . ."

"And what?"

"The crate is filled with rocks and sand."

A wry grin crept across Richard's face. "I want to see Wilhelm's expression."

David handed over the binoculars. "You said you moved the treasure, but I didn't know you emptied them from the crates."

Richard watched Wilhelm as he flailed his arms and screamed at everyone in his presence. Fists clenched, he shook them at the sky.

Satisfied with Wilhelm's tirade, Richard put down the binoculars and turned to David. "I thought you would've known what I meant."

"The least you could've done was let me know *where* you put the treasure. We're partners here, remember?"

"Slight miscommunication on my part," Richard said. "I was in a hurry to see if my idea about transporting the treasure back into the fort was actually a viable one. I apologize for not telling you earlier. It's just that I was a little too focused on the next thing we needed to do."

"So, where is all the treasure?"

"I dumped it into a massive trough at Sandeep's neighbor's house. They had a cow outside, and I figured it would be the last place anyone would look."

"Until the cow eats all the gold and jewels. Then what?"

"I covered it up well. The cow and its owner will have no idea what is hidden beneath the hay."

David cocked his head to the side and pursed his lips. "And how long did you plan to leave the treasure there?"

"Not long. In fact, I think now is about the time we need to go retrieve it."

"With what?"

"I'll show you."

They waited until they were sure the Reichswehr troops had dispersed, creating a safer opportunity to return to the hiding spot. Richard led David to the house and ripped a burlap sack off a large object in the corner of the courtyard.

"Where did you get this cart from?" David asked.

"I borrowed it from Sandeep."

"Did you ask him?"

"There wasn't time. Besides, we've paid him enough already that he can buy a hundred carts if he wants to."

David sighed. "This is asking for trouble, you know. We need to remain as discreet as possible while on these assignments. Stealing people's possessions isn't exactly the best way to operate."

"I'm *borrowing* it," Richard said. "I'm going to return it."

"Never mind. Let's just get out of here before someone sees us."

The city had grown considerably quieter as the festive mood that swept over Jaipur drifted away as most families retreated inside for the night. Several people shuffled along the alley just off the courtyard, but no one seemed to mind or even notice Richard and David scooping out a fortune from a feeding trough.

They took ten minutes to complete the task. Richard reminded David to tighten his *pagri*before they embarked on their perilous journey. After taking turns inspecting one another, David was satisfied they didn't look overly suspicious. He eased behind the handles, volunteering to pull their loot first. As they trudged forward, Richard walked alongside and smoothed out the sack used to hide the jewels and coins. He checked for any areas where the corner was turned up and could reveal the contents of their precious cargo.

"This is absolutely ludicrous," David said.

"What other options do we have?" Richard asked. "We can't very well hide out here forever."

"That would be preferable to this."

"I know this plan is risky, but it's worth it," Richard said. "The moment Germany is able to build a strong military force, the world becomes unstable again."

"You don't need to tell me that," David said. "I'm still

dealing with the consequences of the war that just ended, all thanks to the Germans and their ambitious military."

"The world we're living in is changing rapidly," Richard said. "Who knows what another war would look like with all the new machines and other weaponry? But I predict that it will only become dangerous for both those on the frontlines and those at home. That's why this mission is so important."

"We're only delaying the inevitable," David said.

"Were you always this positive?"

A faint smile appeared on David's lips as he glanced over his shoulder at Richard. "I was once idealistic and optimistic like you."

"What happened?"

"You'll find out when you've been at this job long enough."

After a few minutes of walking along in silence, Richard looked down at his leg when he felt something tugging at it. He stopped and stooped to pick up Smita.

"What are you doing out here?" Richard asked.

David sighed and shook his head. "Not that monkey again. He's been more trouble than he's worth."

"Don't listen to him," Richard said, looking at Smita. "He's got a bee in his bonnet tonight."

Smita flashed his trademark grin and wriggled free before perching on Richard's shoulder.

"Shall we continue?" Richard asked, extending his hand forward.

David didn't say a word as he yanked on the handles and resumed their course. They plodded along for another five minutes before entering the market square, which was mostly shuttered but still had a few evening vendors selling their goods. As they neared the produce section, Richard heard someone yelling behind them. Instead of stopping, David forged ahead, acting as if he either didn't care or didn't hear. Richard, however, glanced over his shoulder and noticed a constable sprinting toward them.

"I think we have some company," Richard said.

"Better think of something quick because we can't outrun anyone while lugging this cart around," David said. "And I'm not about to leave it in the street."

"That might not be the worst thing we could do."

"Don't even think about it," David snapped.

Richard scanned the street and noticed a familiar face from the Reichswehr unit leaning against a wall that served as the main entrance to the market. Behind them, the constable waved his arms as he ran, remaining on a collision course with the two American operatives.

"If you've got any ideas," David said, "now would be a good time to share them."

"I'm thinking," Richard growled, frustrated that he had been unable to engineer an escape plan that allowed them to keep all their goals intact.

CHAPTER 26

THE CONSTABLE PUT HIS HANDS ON HIS KNEES AND struggled to catch his breath as Richard and David finally heeded the officer's calls. Richard eyed the portly man closely as he stood upright. His belly drooped over his belt a couple inches, and his cheeks appeared flushed. If the Reichswehr agent wasn't positioned where he was, Richard believed he and David could outrun the man with ease, even while pulling the cart.

"The English language isn't that hard to understand," the constable said as he narrowed his eyes, the focus of which shifted back and forth between the faces of his two suspects.

Richard cocked his head and pointed at his ear. Mouth agape, he furrowed his brow and gazed at the man. Smita remained perched on Richard's left shoulder.

"You'll have to excuse my friend," David said, mustering up his best British accent as he followed Richard's lead. "He has very poor hearing and relies upon me to instruct him on what to do. I was so focused on getting to our destination that I didn't hear your calling for us."

The constable placed his hands on his hips. "And where might you be headed, pulling a cart like that at this time of night?"

"I'm making my final delivery, sir," David said.

The constable gestured toward David's clothing. "Why are you dressed like that? It's clear you're from England."

"Just trying to fit in."

"If I didn't know any better, I'd say you were trying to disguise yourselves."

"What on Earth for?" David asked. "That'd be a foolish thing to do with those rebellious Americans running wild around the city."

"Who told you about that?" the constable demanded.

"Everyone is talking about them, especially since a bounty has been placed on their heads. I'm surprised someone hasn't already turned them in."

The constable eyed David closely. "What do you have under that blanket?"

"Our delivery," David said.

Richard took his eyes off the conversation for a moment as Smita jumped down to hustle over to a nearby cart brimming with oranges.

"Mind if I take a look?" the constable asked as he grabbed the corner of the cover.

"I'd rather you didn't," David said. "I doubt you want to get bitten by a cobra."

"Don't try to be cheeky with me. I've been watching this cart, and I've yet to see any movement."

David took a step back and looked wide-eyed at the cart. "It's your funeral, mate."

The constable sneered as he prepared to expose what David and Richard had hidden in the rickshaw. But just as the officer looked down, an orange smacked him on the side of his face. He whipped his head in the direction where the fruit came from.

"What the—" he said as he noticed Smita perched atop a mountain of stacked oranges and grinning between screeches.

Smita picked up another orange and hurled it at the constable. Five oranges later, a moment of sudden annoyance simmered over into a roiling rage.The officer darted toward the animal, swearing and promising a dreadful future.

Richard nodded knowingly at David as they seized their opportunity to escape. After dragging the cart behind one of the nearby produce stands, they crouched low and watched from around the corner as Smita screeched with delight and danced around the market to avoid capture. Following about a minute of teasing, Smita ran down the street in the same direction from which they'd come with the officer in pursuit.

"Let's go," David said.

Richard grabbed the rickshaw's handles before glancing toward the market entrance. The Reichswehr agent was gone.

"Looks like we've got a clear path," Richard said.

They hustled along the road, exiting the area as they ventured down a nearly empty street. A few turns later, they were on the road leading to the Thomas Cook & Son's stables near the base of the fort's entry ramp.

Richard and David guided the treasure to safety, stashing their cart behind several bales of hay stacked up behind the barn used to house a variety of the tourist company's pack animals. With the gates locked and no employees present, David convinced Richard to wait until morning to load the jewels on the animals.

"I know we could both use a few hours of sleep," David said.

Richard didn't argue. He took his *pagri* and created a makeshift pillow out of it. Several minutes later, he and David were fast asleep on the ground out of plain sight.

* * *

EARLY THE NEXT MORNING A ROOSTER CROWING STARTLED Richard awake. He pushed himself off the ground and squinted at the sun's first rays streaming over the mountains. David moaned as he twisted from his side to his back.

"Keep quiet," Richard whispered as he placed his hand on David's leg. "Someone is here."

David shot straight up and rubbed his eyes.

"Good morning, sunshine," Richard said. "Ready to finish this mission?"

"I'll do anything for a good night of sleep."

"How about try not to look like you just spent the night on the ground," Richard whispered, gesturing toward David's shirt. "At least brush the dirt off yourself."

David glanced down at his attire and complied with Richard's suggestion. "Now how do I look? Presentable?"

Richard put his finger to his lips. "Stay here while I go coerce that man to let us groom the elephants." He tied his *pagri* and smoothed out some of the wrinkles in his shirt before stepping out from behind the bales.

The door to the stables had been flung wide open. Inside, a man worked his brush methodically down an elephant's hide. He scowled once he noticed Richard walking toward the barn.

"That's quite an animal you've got there," Richard said.

"Who are you? And how'd you get inside?" the man asked.

Richard shrugged. "The gate was open, so I thought I'd come inside and ask if I could do something I've always wanted to do."

"And what's that?"

"Groom an elephant."

The man chuckled. "You need to find new goals. I'd gladly give up this awful job in a heartbeat."

"Would you?" Richard asked, his eyes widening with excitement. "I mean, could I groom this elephant?"

"What about four of them?" the man asked, nodding toward the other animals still secured in their pens.

"What if I gave you ten pounds to let me and a friend groom these beautiful beasts?"

The man furrowed his brow. "What's the catch?"

"There is no catch," Richard said. "We pay you ten pounds to let us do your job. Just let us take over while you take a short walk. And when you come back? Voila! Your job will be finished."

The man offered his hand. "I'm William Saxby, and that sounds like a deal to me."

Richard shook it and then slipped William the cash. He smiled before turning toward the main gate.

"See you in half an hour, William," Richard said.

Once William exited the ground, Richard called for David. He emerged from behind the bales of hay, lugging the rickshaw.

"You made that look rather easy," David said. "It's like you have experience with this sort of thing."

Richard winked. "Let's just say I've got a knack at convincing people to let me do what I want. And enticing him with money didn't hurt either."

David parked the cart inside the stables, and the two men went to work in tandem. They brushed down each elephant then placed the ornate saddle blankets over the animals' back once finished. They dumped a portion of the treasure into the side pouches, making sure the weight was distributed evenly. Then they moved efficiently, completing the task just as William returned.

"I'm impressed," William said as he inspected the elephants. "Are you interested in a job? I'm sure Thomas

Cook & Son would be more than willing to pay you to do this rather than you paying me."

"I've always been fascinated by Hannibal's crossing of the Alps on these beautiful creatures, and I just wanted to spend some time with one of them up close," Richard said. "But if you don't mind, I can watch them for you when they reach the entrance to the fort."

William shook his head. "I don't know. It's one thing to let you groom the elephants in the stable, but up there. . ."

"I'll pay you another ten pounds," Richard said.

"Sure," William said as he held out his hand. "We can make that happen."

Richard inspected the saddle blankets one final time to make sure the jewels and gold coins were all sufficiently hidden from plain sight before heading toward the gate. David lugged the rickshaw behind, insisting that he be pulled up the long sloping entrance to the castle by Richard.

"I think we need a paying customer or two," Richard said. "We will look far less suspicious if we're actually carrying people."

"It was worth a shot," David said with a faint smile.

At the foot of the ramp, Richard asked an elderly couple if they would prefer a ride to the gate rather than trudging up the hill themselves. They both agreed to ride and promptly sat down. Upon reaching the top, the couple thanked Richard for his assistance and charged inside the fort.

"Now we wait," Richard said as he peered down the meandering ramp leading to the gates.

A half hour later, the first Thomas Cook & Son elephant lumbered up the hill with a pair of men onboard. After they dismounted and entered the gates, Richard approached William.

"Time for us to get to work?" Richard asked.

William held out a brush. "She's all yours."

Richard signaled for David, and he strolled over pulling the cart. With the elephant positioned next to the wall, Richard led her out a few feet to give them enough room to work. David held up a burlap sack, while Richard cut a slit in the bottom of the saddle blanket, allowing the jewels and coins to pour out. As soon as they were finished, another elephant arrived and they repeated the process over again. Four animals later, Richard and David had transferred all the treasure into two large burlap sacks and were set to enter Fort Jaigahr.

"Are you ready?" Richard asked.

David nodded. "I can't wait for this operation to be over. I'm beginning to develop an even stronger disdain for the Germans, which I didn't think was possible."

"Well, keep your head down then," Richard said. "I just saw Wilhelm and Reinhard."

David cursed and clenched his fists. "I swear if they ruin this whole thing now—"

"Don't forget we're the ones wanted by the authorities here, not them."

"Don't remind me," David said.

"Just stay calm," Richard said. "We're just two guys giving rides to tourists."

Richard and David prepared to enter the fort and return the treasure to a hiding place—albeit a different one. But before they took a step inside, Richard heard an all-too-familiar voice shout from across the courtyards.

"There are the Americans! Get them!"

Wincing, Richard didn't need to turn around to know Wilhelm had spotted him.

"Time for plan B," Richard said.

CHAPTER 27

Wilhelm was certain that at least one of the veins in his neck had exploded as his pulse surged, incited by both his anger and his passionate quest to capture the treasure his Reichswehr troops had found. Just twenty-four hours earlier, he'd thought his unit of special forces had scored their first big discovery after getting foiled in Egypt. But somehow, Richard Halliburton had managed to thwart a master plan of recovery and escape to the homeland without Indian authorities being the wiser. And Wilhelm had to use every ounce of restraint he possessed to keep from murdering his nemesis in broad daylight.

Instead of waiting on any of his soldiers to initiate the pursuit, Wilhelm realized he needed to play the Americans' game if he was going to catch them. Richard and his colleague had wrestled away the reins of a pair of horses from a nearby tour guide. The brief confrontation lasted no more than a few seconds as the man was overpowered by the American agents. Each man secured a burlap sack in his lap before digging his heels into newly acquired steeds and racing down the ramp.

Wilhelm rushed toward another nearby tour guide who was just cresting the top of the hill with a pair of customers on horseback. Instead of waiting for the people to dismount,

Wilhelm yanked the two people off as they tumbled to the ground. He put one foot in the stirrup and hoisted himself into the saddle.

"Come on," he shouted. "Let's go."

Wilhelm clutched the reins tightly as his horse reared back before galloping after Richard Halliburton. As Wilhelm expertly guided his horse around the sharp curves of the path filled with a half dozen switchbacks, he dodged oncoming elephants and rickshaw riders clattering along the trail. After a few minutes, he heard thunderous hooves thumping the ground. He looked back and noticed Reinhard was bearing down on his commander along with three other Reichswehr soldiers fanned out and trailing their junior leader.

"I thought you'd never make it," Wilhelm said.

"You need to have more faith in us than that," Reinhard said. "These men are loyal to you to a fault."

"And you?" Wilhelm asked.

"I think we're all willing to make the kind of sacrifice necessary to restore Germany to her rightful place in this world," Reinhard said.

Instead of taking a moment to be proud of Reinhard's courage and willingness to sacrifice himself for his country, Wilhelm could only think about the letter in his pocket and how a truly good leader would've never withheld the information it contained. He shrugged off the thought in an attempt to stay focused on the most pressing matter facing him and his team: catching Richard Halliburton.

As they reached the valley floor, Wilhelm directed his men to split up, sending three of them around the outer perimeter of the city, while he and Reinhard charged toward the marketplace.

"We'll meet back in half an hour at the police station," Wilhelm said before the groups parted ways.

Wilhelm scanned the area for the two Americans, counting on them to try to disappear in a crowded place. With the rest of the city on the lookout for them in hopes of earning a significant reward, their options were extremely limited, especially with the treasure in tow.

"Look," Reinhard said as he pointed across the market. "Aren't those the horses they were using?"

Wilhelm nodded as he eased toward the two animals tied up outside a restaurant located just off the main street.

"Stay alert," Wilhelm said. "They've got to be around here somewhere."

Wilhelm strode up to the owner and asked if he'd seen the two Americans.

"If I had, I wouldn't be standing here," the man said. "I would've taken them to a constable."

"You're sure you haven't seen them?" Reinhard asked. "These are the horses they were riding a few minutes ago."

"Trust me," the owner said. "For two hundred pounds, I would've found the strength to muscle both of them to the ground. There's not much they could've enticed me with to keep me quiet."

"Except more money," Wilhelm said under his breath.

"If I see them, I'll let the authorities know."

Wilhelm turned and lumbered toward the market. Weaving in and out of the constant foot traffic, he did his best to avoid the onslaught of oncoming shoppers and storekeepers. The clothes that the two U.S. agents were wearing made it difficult to pick them out in a crowd. From behind, the city's entire male population didn't look all that different. The backs of turbans and white shirts, jackets, and cloaks didn't offer any identifying marks. After a few minutes, he finally stopped and strained to see around the crowd, searching for anyone acting out of the ordinary.

"They've got to be around here somewhere," Wilhelm said.

"If I wanted to disappear, this is where I'd go," Reinhard said.

"They'll have to leave at some point."

"It might be too late by then," Reinhard said. "We need to find them right now before they figure out a way to get the treasure out of the city. Catching them without the jewels might as well be a failure."

"It *will* be a failure," Wilhelm said. "We need to stay sharp and continue our search."

Wilhelm sauntered over to a vendor and purchased a pair of cloths to make pangris for himself and Reinhard. In a matter of seconds, Wilhelm managed to swirl up the material to create an authentic headpiece. Then he did the same for Reinhard.

"We'll be more difficult to see coming," Wilhelm said. "Now, let's keep moving."

Wilhelm ordered Reinhard to the other side of the market so they could split up and cover more ground. They drifted along and inspected the scene, casting a watchful eye on anything that appeared out of the usual. Several minutes later, Wilhelm stumbled upon a couple men huddled in a tight alley with two woven baskets. He signaled for Reinhard to circle around the outside. After a quick nod, Reinhard rushed across the market and down another connected narrow passageway.

Wilhelm drew his gun and kept it trained on the ground just in case his hunch was proven wrong. As he neared the two men, he shouted at them.

"Keep your hands where I can see them," he said.

One of the men turned around and stared wide-eyed at Wilhelm. Nearly all the color had vanished from the man's face, and his lips trembled as he spoke.

"I'm sorry," he said. "We didn't mean any harm. We were just—"

Wilhelm held out his hand, gesturing for the man to stop. "Have you seen two suspicious men run by here recently? Men dressed just like you?"

They eyed Wilhelm carefully and then glanced at each other. "About five minutes ago, I saw a pair of men run along the alley parallel to this one just west of the main market street."

"That has to be them," Reinhard said.

Wilhelm wasn't sure if the men were telling the truth or if they were simply trying to end the surprise encounter. But in the end, it didn't matter. Richard had vanished into the bustle of Jaipur's major vein of commerce. Chasing him down was better than standing in front of two quaking thieves who were desperate to get on with their day. If Wilhelm was moving, he figured he exponentially increased his odds of finding Richard and his cohort.

Signaling for Reinhard to follow, Wilhelm hustled through the marketplace again, searching for the location where he'd been directed.

"You look south of this intersection," Wilhelm instructed.

Reinhard nodded. "We need to get more men in here and expand our search."

Wilhelm shook his head. "We don't need anyone else's help. If we do a thorough search, we should be able to flush them into the open. They can't hide here forever."

The men rummaged through baskets and peered beneath blanketed items as they circled a small portion of the market. One by one, each promising arrest turned into dead end after dead end. Wherever the American operatives had gone, it was becoming clearer that it wasn't anywhere near the epicenter of Jaipur.

Several minutes later, Wilhelm and Reinhard rejoined at the designated spot where they'd started from.

"No sign of them," Reinhard said. "I'm beginning to think these two men don't exist."

"But their horses are here," Wilhelm said. "They couldn't have gone far."

Wilhelm led Reinhard back to the main marketplace as they scanned the crowded spot, now filling rapidly with shop owners returning from lunch. Despite the crush of humanity essentially freezing Wilhelm to his location, he glanced near one of the basket-making businesses several tables down.

"Come on," Wilhelm said, motioning for Reinhard to follow.

The men hustled through the crowd, shifting sideways to avoid smashing into others. After a vigorous dance through the mayhem, they found two men huddled over in the corner, nearly out of sight as they held up a burlap sack and dumped it into one of the baskets.

"We'll take it from here," Wilhelm said, certain that he'd apprehended the right pair of men. When they turned around and looked up at him, he realized he'd done just that. A faint smile crept across his lips.

"Well, Mr. Halliburton, looks like your luck has run out," Wilhelm said.

Richard and his associate dashed down the alley, bumping everyone in their path as they attempted a getaway. However, when they reached the next intersection, three members of the Reichswehr unit blocked their way. They seized the American agents and marched them back toward Wilhelm, who remained standing by the basket.

"Mr. Halliburton, you are quite the worthy adversary, but your attempts to derail our mission have come to an end," Wilhelm said.

"Are you going to kill us right here in the street?" Richard asked. "Because if you aren't, this is far from over."

Wilhelm glanced around and noticed that a sizeable crowd had gathered to watch. Eliminating Richard and his colleague would be preferable for the long term, but in the immediate future such a move could have the kind of repercussions that Wilhelm sought to avoid.

"There doesn't need to be any blood shed today," Wilhelm said. "You tried to steal precious treasures from Fort Jaigahr, historical artifacts that belong to all these wonderful people here in India. And now we're going to restore it to them."

"I don't know what you're talking about," Richard said with a sneer.

"Open this basket," Wilhelm said.

Richard eyed the German leader closely. "I don't know if I want to do that."

"I'm not going to ask you again," Wilhelm said as he leaned closer to the straw basket.

"Don't say I didn't warn you." Richard ripped the lid off.

A cobra popped up and hissed at Wilhelm before striking at him. With wide eyes, he jumped back. The snake lunged toward him again.

"Put it back," Wilhelm ordered.

"I warned you," Richard said while complying with Wilhelm's command.

Once the snake was secure, Wilhelm placed his hands on Richard's shoulders. "Where's the treasure?"

Richard shrugged. "I don't know what you're talking about."

"This is your last chance before I turn both of you over to the authorities here to deal with you for your previous theft charges. Now, where is the treasure?"

Neither man answered as Wilhelm grew more furious by the second. When he realized they weren't going to say anything, he looked at Reinhard.

"Let's not turn these gentlemen over to the authorities just yet," Wilhelm said. "I have a few more questions for them."

CHAPTER 28

Richard refused to cooperate with the Reichswehr agents who shoved him against the wall as they bound him and David with ropes. Wilhelm had to get involved, putting his shoulder into Richard's back in order to pin him back. With his face smashed against the wall, he glanced beyond the Germans to notice a sizeable crowd watching the proceedings with keen interest.

"I'm an innocent man," Richard said. "Whatever these men are accusing me of is a lie. I've done nothing wrong."

"I thought we were trying to keep a low profile," David said.

"Shut up," Wilhelm said, switching his pressure from Richard's back to his head. "You will have your chance to speak your piece. In the meantime, I advise you to stay quiet, if anything for the sake of your health."

Wilhelm yanked Richard's head back a few inches before jamming it against the wall again. Richard grimaced in pain but remained quiet.

"Seems like you're a quick learner, Mr. Halliburton," Wilhelm said. "Let's go have a chat some place more private."

The Reichswehr agents ushered their two prisoners down the alley, pushing through the onlookers clogging the passageway. They reached a wider street and walked for several minutes, weaving back and forth until reaching a house with a freshly painted wooden door. Richard noted that in comparison to the other neighborhood homes, this one appeared far more kempt.

Once inside, they were greeted by a couple Reichswehr agents. Richard had been taking count of just how many he'd seen in Jaipur—and it seemed they were growing in number. Immediately, a pair of men escorted Richard and David into the basement, which was little more than a bare room with a dirt floor. After their pockets were emptied, the men flung Richard and David forward. They stumbled to the ground and came to a stop in a dusty heap.

"Don't get any ideas," one of the men said. "Someone will be along shortly to have a nice little chat with you."

Following that terse statement, the men spun and ascended the stairs before disappearing from sight.

"I'm hoping this wasn't part of your plan," David said.

"Stuffing that snake into the basket didn't quite workout the way I'd hoped," Richard said. "We were supposed to use that in an open area, not in closed-off quarters. But I didn't really have a choice, did I?"

"What's done is done," David said. "I'm not going to joke with you about it too much, especially since I'm not certain we're going to survive the night."

"What's keeping us alive right now—not to mention out of a British prison—is the fact that Wilhelm doesn't know where the jewels are."

"And neither do we, if we're being entirely honest."

"We'll be able to retrieve them," Richard said. "In the meantime, we need to get out of here in a hurry."

Before they could plot their escape, Richard heard the hinges squeak on the door at the top of the stairs, followed by heavy footfalls on the steps. The source of the slow and steady thumping eventually came into view—Karl Wilhelm. He wore a sly smile with his hands clasped behind his back. Coming to a stop in front of Richard, Wilhelm ordered his prisoners to stand up, but neither complied.

"We can do this the easy way or the hard way," Wilhelm said. "It's your choice."

"I prefer you just ignore us since we aren't going to tell you anything," Richard said.

"I'm not so sure I can ignore you," Wilhelm said. "You have something that belongs to me, and I want it back."

"First of all, it's not yours," David said. "And secondly, what makes you think we would tell you anything?"

Wilhelm tilted his head back and looked down his nose at David. "I'm quite confident in my methods of interrogation. Just apply the right amount of pressure to the most tender of spots and you can usually get what you're after."

"I hate to break it to you," Richard said, "but we don't exactly have any tender spots. We're mostly covered with callouses from the rough journeys we've been on. It's what gives us character, the kind of character that will sit here with steely resolve and let you know that even your fiercest interrogation tactics will result in a failure."

Wilhelm lowered his head, jamming his forehead up against Richard's. "You talk a good game, but it counts as nothing but idle chatter now. You're in my domain, and I'm going to get you to tell me what I want to know—or else you're going to pay a steep price."

Richard narrowed his eyes and glared at Wilhelm. "I invite you to try."

Wilhelm withdrew and spun toward the door. He stopped just before exiting and looked back at Richard and David.

"When I return, you'll experience a wrath unlike any other," Wilhelm said before vanishing up the stairs.

Moments later, the soldier guarding Richard and David also eased up the steps and left the two Americans alone. Richard felt the hole being bored into him by David's eyes.

"Is there any reason for you to stare at me like that while you're seething?" Richard asked.

David spoke in a slow and measured pace. "Are you out of your mind?"

"You ask me that so much that I'm beginning to wonder if perhaps one of us actually is," Richard said.

"You've only irritated Wilhelm further with your bravado shtick. He's going to come down on us hard—or quite possibly kill us—thanks to your inability to keep your mouth shut."

"As long as he doesn't have the treasure, we're fine," Richard said. "And he needs us to get it, which is an inescapable fact."

"What's also inescapable is this dungeon they've put us in."

"It certainly appears that way, though I'm not inclined to accept that as fact just yet."

David sighed. "This isn't some fantastical fairy world we're living in right now. It's very real—as is our danger. You can't simply wish things away or pretend like they're different than they are. I'm sorry that no one told you this before you agreed to serve with Army Intelligence, but what we do matters. And the consequences for our mistakes can be grave for ourselves and others."

"Are you finished?" Richard asked.

David nodded and hung his head, kicking at the dirt floor.

"Good, because I have a knife, and all I need to do is figure out a way to use it."

"You have a knife?" David asked, his mouth falling agape. "They stripped us down and took everything out of our pockets."

"Mine wasn't in my pocket," Richard said. "It's in my belt buckle."

"What on Earth?"

"I can't show it to you now because my hands are tied behind my back, but if you help me get it, I can cut us free and get out of here."

Richard explained how to release the blade from the buckle. David stood with his back to Richard's chest and followed his directions. In a matter of seconds, David was holding the knife. He gripped the handle tightly as Richard turned back to back with David and cut through the rope. Once free, they devised a scheme to break out of their prison.

Richard stood at the bottom of the stairs with his hand tied loosely behind his back and called for the guard.

"Please, sir," Richard said. "I need to relieve myself, and I'm afraid that's impossible since my hands are tied behind me. Would you be so kind to help me?"

After a few seconds, the door swung open and one of the Reichswehr agents lumbered down the steps while clutching a dagger.

"You two are more trouble than you're worth," he said before muttering a few curse words in German.

When he reached the bottom step, Richard turned his back so the man could untie him. The guard chuckled.

"You don't expect me to cut you free, do you?" he asked. "Wilhelm would kill me. Go stand in the corner, and I'll drop your trousers for you." Then he turned to David, pointing the knife at him. "And you stay right where you are."

Richard complied with the guard's orders and marched toward one corner and waited. When the guard reached around to unbuckle Richard's pants, David crashed into the German, slamming him into the wall. Before he knew what hit him, Richard and David had knocked the man unconscious. They stripped him of his gun and knife then secured him with ropes before quietly heading upstairs.

At the top, they found another Reichswehr operative sitting in the kitchen with his feet propped up and reading a book. He didn't look up when he asked a question in German.

Richard nodded knowingly at David and they rushed the man, hitting him several times in the face before he had a chance to fight back. With their captors out cold and stripped of their guns, Richard and David armed themselves and eased through the rest of the house. After they were satisfied that no one else was here, they slipped out the back door and tried to get their bearings.

"We need to get back to the market to find that woman," Richard said.

David agreed, and they started their trip through Jaipur in search of the lady who had agreed to hide their two burlap sacks.

"Maybe it was a mistake not to tell her what was in them," David said. "Because by now, I'm sure she was wondering what was so important and has probably looked by now."

"I wouldn't be so sure," Richard said. "She seemed like the honest type."

"And what makes you think you can just look at a person and tell if they're being straight with you or not?"

"I did run with quite a crew of characters at Princeton. You wouldn't believe some of the ways those rascals behaved at times. I had a good training ground there."

David sighed. "Princeton is a long way from India and vastly different, in case you haven't noticed."

"People are people," Richard said. "But if you felt so strongly about this, perhaps you should've voiced your concerns before we handed over an enormous fortune to her."

"We didn't have a choice. We were fortunate the Reichswehr troops passed right by us the first time and didn't see us when we were making that initial exchange."

"You always need a bit of good luck in whatever you do if you're going to succeed, particularly if your success hinges upon evading capture."

David cocked his head and looked at Richard. "You seem to have an inordinate amount of experience getting away from people. Do you feel like this is normal?"

Richard laughed. "When you're the worst rascal in a gang of them, it becomes a regular part of life."

A smile crept over David's lips as he shook his head. "And it seems as though you haven't changed."

Richard nodded. "There's something strangely freeing about getting into mischief for your country."

"At the moment, I'll settle for keeping these jewels out of the hands of the Germans and getting home in one piece."

"It's never easy, is it?"

They plodded along until they reached the market place. Striding up to the kiosk where they met the woman who'd stashed the treasure for them, Richard stared wide-eyed at an elderly gentleman standing there in her place.

"Would you gentlemen be interested in any of our baskets?" he asked.

Richard furrowed his brow. "There was a woman working here earlier named Sarita. Do you perhaps know where she went?"

The man shook his head. "I'm afraid you must be mistaken. This is my store—and I'm the only one who has been here all day."

CHAPTER 29

WILHELM RETURNED TO THE REICHSWEHR'S makeshift headquarters with both Reinhard and Ludwig in tow. After discussing the appropriate way to pressure Richard Halliburton and his accomplice into giving up the location of the treasure, Wilhelm was itching to get to work. However, his anticipation quickly gave way to outrage when he saw two of his agents bound on the kitchen floor.

"Where are they?" Wilhelm demanded.

"They left a half hour ago," one of the men said.

"What happened?" Wilhelm asked before putting his hand in the air. "Never mind. It's obvious they pulled one over on you imbeciles. I asked Seeckt to send me some of the best men he had available to replace the other agents I'd lost, and this is what I get. Neither of you are worthy to be a part of my *wolfsrudel*."

Wilhelm kicked a wooden chair, splintering it against the wall.

"Sir, we'll find them," Reinhard said. "They can't get out of the city using the trains—and it's obvious they were trying to hide the treasure somewhere in the fort. Now that they can't do either of those things, they're in quite a predicament."

"Let's make sure of that," Wilhelm said. "I want you to spread the word that I'm offering five hundred pounds for their capture."

"Five hundred pounds? But, sir, you just can't—"

"Don't tell me what I can and can't do. I want every man, woman, child, monkey, donkey, elephant, and cow in Jaipur to be overturning every stone in search of these American agents. Five hundred pounds will definitely stir the interest of everyone with a pulse. If we're lucky, we might even have some fortune hunters pour into Jaipur to assist with the hunt."

"But where are you going to get that kind of money?" Reinhard asked. "You know Seeckt won't be happy to see our resources drained like that."

"Seeckt won't care when he looks at this fortune," Wilhelm said. "He'll throw me a parade right down the middle of Berlin."

"We're a long way from parades," Ludwig said. "We need to find those two thieves and make them pay."

Wilhelm nodded. "Go make it happen. And, Reinhard, you're with me."

Ludwig untied the two men on the floor before they darted toward the door.

"Don't you dare disappoint me again like that," Wilhelm called out as they hustled away.

Reinhard sat down. "I'm sorry, sir. I thought those two men would've been competent enough to hold Mr. Halliburton and his associate for at least an hour."

"No, it's my fault," Wilhelm said as he grabbed a couple glasses from the cabinet along with a bottle of brandy. "I should've never left and just sent you to secure Ludwig and our secret weapons. I lacked the confidence in my skills to extract a confession, and I have no one to blame but myself now."

"Sir, it's quite understandable. We're still dealing with an enemy that we know very little about. From every report I've read, Mr. Halliburton is little more than a vagabond who's in the middle of wandering across Europe, Africa, and Asia with no real purpose. None of our agents in Berlin have ever heard of him. The dossier we have on him was literally cobbled together overnight when we first encountered Mr. Halliburton—and there's nothing new to report according to the intelligence briefing sent by telegram yesterday."

"How are we supposed to deal with this man?"

"Quickly and discreetly."

Wilhelm took a swig from his glass. "If he goes missing, we might incite the ire of the Americans. And the last thing we want is for them to be more closely inspecting our adherence to the Treaty of Versailles. Our presence here is enough to let them know that we're operating outside the bounds of that agreement."

"Yes, but no official complaint has been lodged yet, which would seem to suggest that the Americans don't want word to get out that they're tracking us. That would communicate a serious mistrust among their foreign allies, who are still clueless regarding our presence abroad."

"Exactly," Wilhelm said, "which means we can handle them in whatever manner we choose. If the American government was going to say something, they already would have. And they certainly wouldn't out themselves now after losing a pair of agents in the field and, along with them, a method of tracking our team."

"So, we're back to quickly and discreetly?" Reinhard asked.

"Quickly and discreetly," Wilhelm said before throwing back the rest of his drink. "Once we find them, we eliminate them."

"Let me handle this for you," Reinhard said. "I'll make sure there aren't any mistakes."

"Very well then," Wilhelm said. "I'll leave their disposal in your very capable hands."

"Are you ready to go back to the market, sir?" Reinhard asked.

"Let's go."

Wilhelm and Reinhard exited the house, entering the busy streets which bustled with more activity in the afternoon. Men pulling carts squeezed past one another, while other merchants drifted in and out of the throng of women searching for ingredients for their evening meals.

After meandering through the people for a few minutes, Wilhelm felt the buzz in the air. The excitement seemed almost palpable. He was certain the atmosphere was due to the large reward he'd offered, but he wanted to make sure his hunch was correct.

"What is everyone talking about?" Wilhelm asked a man leaning against a wall.

"There's a reward out for two Americans," the man said. "Five hundred pounds!"

"Five hundred?"

The man nodded. "That's right. Five hundred pounds. If these owners felt comfortable enough to close up their shops to go search for those two thieves, I'm certain we would be the only people standing here in a matter of minutes."

"Well, why don't they?"

"Why don't they do what?" the man asked.

"Close up their shops and hunt for the pair of Americans?"

He shrugged. "I don't know. The idea of getting five hundred pounds is enough to get everyone talking, but only some people to spring into action. But a thousand pounds?

If the reward was raised that high, I'm sure everyone in this country would begin hunting for them."

Wilhelm eyed the man closely then glanced at Reinhard, who subtly shook his head. "It's disappointing to hear that. Money shouldn't be what motivates us to take action."

"Then what should?"

"Desire," Wilhelm said.

"Or fear," the man added. "If the two Americans were murderers instead of thieves, I'm sure more people would join the search."

"If you only knew," Wilhelm said under his breath before nodding at the man as they veered down a side street.

"What is your name?" Wilhelm asked.

"Manish," the man said. "And I make the best curry in all of Jaipur. Come see me in the market sometime."

"Perhaps I will," Wilhelm said.

A few minutes later, another man rushed up to Wilhelm.

"Are you the man paying the ransom for the two Americans?"

Wilhelm shrugged. "Why do you ask?"

"Because I know who they've been working with and where to find her."

"Her?" Wilhelm questioned as he cocked his head to the side.

The man nodded. "So, are you the person I'm looking for?"

"You've found him," Wilhelm said. "Now lead me to the two Americans and the reward is yours."

The man broke into a wide grin before spinning around and striking off toward the eastern side of the city.

Wilhelm also began to smile. Five hundred pounds was more than enough to properly motivate the people of Jaipur. And it wouldn't be long before he exacted retribution on Mr. Halliburton and his colleague—and eliminated them forever.

CHAPTER 30

RICHARD SIGHED AS HE PONDERED WHAT COURSE OF action might lead them to Sarita, the enchantress who David imagined was lavishly spending all the money she'd acquired from them. While Richard knew it wasn't *his* fortune, he wanted to make sure it remained where it belonged—in the hands of the Indian people—instead of being squandered. And David's suggestion that she was probably tossing priceless jewels at street merchants to get what she wanted made Richard cringe.

"How could we have been so stupid?" Richard asked aloud.

David shook his head. "*We*?"

"Yeah, *we* gave her all the treasure, trusting that she'd keep it safe for us."

"No, *you* suggested we give everything to her. This wasn't a discussion in the least bit."

"Okay, perhaps you're right," Richard said. "I may have been a little pushy in wanting to let Sarita watch all the riches for us, but she appeared to be as innocent as they come."

"And yet you boast about your ability to sense the truth about who people really are."

"Sometimes I make mistakes," Richard said, forcing a grin. "Nobody's perfect."

"This wasn't just some mistake. This was a vast fortune that we worked hard to procure, prying it out of the hands of the greedy and vengeful Germans. If the Reichswehr was able to liquidate everything we found into their currency, we would have a burgeoning crisis on our hands. You insisted that this Sarita woman was going to work diligently to ensure no one found out about what we discovered. But instead, she's nowhere to be found—and neither is our treasure."

Richard held up his hands in a gesture to calm a seething David. "I understand you're upset. And so am I, but I'm just choosing to maintain my composure right now.In the worst case scenario, she makes off with the fortune, while the Reichswehr are left empty handed," Richard said. "Besides, you shouldn't get all bent out of shape just yet. We might still find her."

"If I found out what was inside those baskets, I would've stuffed as much as I could into a suitcase and boarded the next train out of here," David said.

Richard shrugged. "Not everyone sees the world the same way you do. You don't know Sarita. Maybe she's an honest soul."

David laughed and shook his head. "I'm not much older than you, but you still have a lot to learn about this world. People aren't nearly as virtuous as you believe them to be. Trust me on this one."

"I suppose you would rather me think the worst about everyone I meet then?"

"That's not what I'm saying. It's just that . . ."

"It's just *what*?" Richard asked.

"This isn't Tennessee, Richard. Not everyone has a heart of gold and a splash of genuine care for their fellow man. In case you haven't noticed, we're in a portion of the world that's only as advanced as it is because of the influence of its occupiers. If England wasn't here, India would be unbearable to visit."

"I refuse to believe the worst about people, no matter how hard you might try to convince me. You go ahead and judge Sarita, but I'm going to withhold any kind of accusations until we find her."

"Which might not ever happen—and you know it."

"Do you think we should just leave?" Richard asked. "Because I certainly won't feel like this mission was a success if we do. I want to see this thing through to the end before meeting back up with Harvey."

"Fine," David said, "we'll keep looking for her. We can't very well fill out a report until we know what's actually happened with all the treasure anyway."

"Excellent. Now I recommend we circle the market several times to see if we missed her somehow. She has to be here."

"Okay, but stay alert," David said. "The Reichswehr agents are everywhere."

Richard and David spent the next half hour slowly moving in and out of the crowd in search of Sarita. A couple times, Richard thought he found her only to be fooled by another woman who held a similar striking appearance. David grew impatient and recommended they look elsewhere.

"But what if she comes back?" Richard asked.

"What if she's already on a train to Calcutta? We could play this game all day long, but it's not going to change the fact she's not here. And the more time that passes, the less hopeful I get that we're going to get back the fortune."

Richard spun to look in the opposite direction when he collided with a man carrying a bucket of hot coals. Jarred loose by the contact, several of them fell to the ground and two of them fell onto Richard's foot. He let out a yelp before crumpling to grab the burned skin. David knelt next to his colleague.

"Are you okay?" he asked.

Richard removed his hand to peek at the wound. The skin had already turned red, and a searing pain throbbed in his foot.

"I'm sorry," the man said. "I didn't see you and. . . Hey, aren't you one of those Americans who—"

"Do I sound like a bloody American?" Richard asked in a feigned English accent, which was good enough to immediately quell any doubts about the origin of his birthplace. "You just dumped blazing coals on me, and all you can think about is getting some reward. Go on."

The man scooped up the remaining coals with a castiron spoon and lumped them back into his bucket. Richard waited for the man to disappear before moving. Once he was gone, Richard attempted to get back on his feet but stumbled again.

"Are you all right?" asked another man who had stopped nearby.

Richard didn't look up as he waved off the man and conjured up his British accent again. "I'll be fine."

"Richard," the man said, "is that you?"

Richard looked above to see Sandeep standing with a basket tucked underneath one arm and his *pangi* in the other.

"Please tell me that lid is fastened tightly," Richard said, realizing it was safe to switch back to his natural speaking voice. "I just got hot coals dumped on my foot. The last thing I need on top of that is a snake bite."

"It *is* you," Sandeep said. "What are you doing out in the open like this? Those German soldiers are still looking for you along with the rest of the city. It's not safe for you to be here."

"In more ways than one apparently," Richard said,

glancing down at his foot. David and Sandeep helped Richard upright.

"Just keep your head down and come with me," Sandeep said. "I'm almost certain the Germans are still watching me."

"Where are you taking us?" David asked.

"I have a friend who runs an apothecary. She'll be able to give Richard something to soothe that burn."

"Are you sure she's trustworthy?" David asked.

"You won't meet a better person," Sandeep said. "I can assure you of that."

They peeled out of the main square and scurried along a road for a few minutes until Sandeep darted down a side street and knocked on a door.

"I'm not sure this is a good idea," David said. "Why don't we stand aside and out of view while you get the balm for Richard's injury?"

Sandeep shrugged. "If you insist."

Richard and David stood with their backs against the wall, heads down to avoid being easily noticed. The door creaked as it opened, and a woman's voice echoed in the alleyway.

"Sandeep, to what do I owe the pleasure of your visit today?" she said.

Richard recognized her immediately. He looked up and strode up behind Sandeep.

"Sarita," Richard said, "we thought you were gone?"

Sarita eyed him carefully before glancing to the left and right. Then she gestured for them to come inside.

"What happened?" she asked once they were all safely in her house.

"It's a burn from hot coals," Richard said. "I was—"

"We have the same question for you," David said. "We were starting to wonder if you'd run off with all our possessions."

"I'm sorry," she said. "I—I had somewhere to be."

"Where are the bags we asked you to take care of for us?" David asked.

She sighed and looked down. "They're—they're some place safe."

"What are you not telling us?" Richard asked. "It's okay, whatever it is."

"Go ahead, Sarita," Sandeep said. "Tell them where you were."

She shuffled across the room toward a table that contained several potted plants. "Let me get something for that burn on your foot."

"Sarita, it's okay," Sandeep said. "They're not going to tell anyone."

"Tell anyone *what?*" David asked.

Sarita turned around and was holding an aloe leaf. Kneeling next to Richard's foot, she cracked open the leaf and applied the soothing balm.

"Where are our bags?" David asked again.

Richard held out his hand, gesturing for David to calm down.

"It's at the leper colony," she said as she looked at the floor. "No one else will go there to tend to their other sicknesses, something I learned when my uncle contracted leprosy. So, I started making regularly scheduled visits twice a week."

"And you've never gotten the disease?" Richard asked.

"I've been doing this for five years now, and I'm completely healthy. But what I do there is a well-kept secret. If anyone found out, my business in the marketplace would be ruined."

"We won't tell a soul," Richard said.

"But what about our bags?" David asked. "We need those back as soon as possible."

"I can't go for another three days," she said. "The women who deliver food to the colony hide me beneath a blanket on their cart. If I were to go up there, someone would see me, and it'd be devastating."

"Then we'll go," Richard said. "Tell us where it's hidden."

"Okay," Sarita said. "I'm so sorry I didn't bring it back with me, but I just couldn't carry it. The bags were too heavy. What was in them?"

"Just some things we found that we're trying to return to the rightful owner," Richard said.

"I'll draw you a map," she said. "But you must wait until night time. The colony is on the site of a dilapidated fort and is guarded by several men to make sure the lepers don't escape. So, the tricky part will be getting out of the fort, not getting into it. And you're going to need the cover of darkness to help you."

The three men watched as Sarita sketched the location of the bags, giving Richard and David detailed instructions on the route to take in order to avoid detection. When she was finished, she rolled up the plans and handed them to David.

"I hope you're able to retrieve them without any incident," she said. "If you think the punishments handed down through British law are severe, I urge you not to test our country's customs when it comes to leprosy. You'll find them to be most unforgiving and inhumane."

"Come," Sandeep said. "I know where we can hide you until nightfall."

The three men strode toward the door, and all but Richard exited. He lingered for a minute on the steps.

"I appreciate what you did for us," Richard said.

"And I appreciate you keeping my secret," Sarita said.

"Of course," Richard said. "Now, there was one other thing I was wondering if you could help us with."

"Anything. Just name it."

Richard smiled. "I think you might actually enjoy this too."

CHAPTER 31

As night fell over Jaipur, Sandeep led Richard and David to the leper colony to retrieve the treasure. The castle was positioned at the edge of a lake, the gates constructed on land, while the rest of the structure was built out over the water. According to Sarita, she hid the bags in a dried out well that had been almost entirely filled in. She covered the top with a board, counting on the fact that no one would even be tempted to look inside.

Explaining while she sketched out the directions, Sarita had said the well was located in a remote area of the castle ruins. However, she stressed getting out presented the stiffest challenge.

"This is as far as I go," Sandeep said.

Richard studied Sandeep closely. "Are you scared of contracting the disease?"

Sandeep nodded. "You don't have leprosy in America?"

Richard shrugged. "I guess I haven't thought about it much. We just send all the lepers to Louisiana."

"And they get cared for there?" Sandeep asked.

"I'm not sure, but I've never been afraid of getting it. I'm far more afraid of the Germans starting another war."

"But if your arms fall off, who cares about war?" Sandeep asked.

"I'm going to pretend like you didn't say that," Richard said. "I'm trying to think positive thoughts here, and you're not helping."

Sandeep smiled. "Don't worry. I'll help you tonight, just as you asked."

"Not a minute before midnight," Richard said. "We'll be ready."

"Good luck," Sandeep said before he patted Richard and David on the back and then spun in the other direction.

Richard peered through his binoculars at the pair of turrets still intact over the steel gate leading inside the fortress.

"What do you see?" David asked.

"Well, Sarita was right about one thing," Richard said. "Those two guards don't care about anyone getting in. They look entirely disinterested in who enters. But I doubt anyone is leaving through those front gates."

"What other options do we have?" David asked.

"From what I can tell, not many. If we weren't attempting to recover such heavy metal objects, I might suggest leaving through the water."

"Well, that's definitely not going to work. Anything else?"

"We need a diversion—and a boat."

David sighed. "And where do you think we're going to get one of those at this time of night?"

Richard shrugged. "I'm sure we can borrow one. There are plenty of them beached on the shore."

"I'm nominating you for that task. The less time I spend in the water, the better."

"Suit yourself," Richard said. "I'm more than happy to handle the arrangements."

"I'll set up the ropes," David said. "Meet me back here in an hour."

* * *

AN HOUR LATER, THE TWO AGENTS RECONVENED. AFTER hiding a fresh pair of clothes given to him by Sandeep, Richard managed to find a seaworthy boat devoid of nets, traps, and lines—all the hallmark supplies of a fisherman's vessel. The particular one he dragged into the water had a faded paint job, and the wood appeared weathered. He paddled out to the far south corner of the castle and tied off there, just below where David had affixed a pair of ropes.

"What did you find out?" Richard asked.

"There's a section on the base of the wall that would be relatively easy to sneak into if we distracted the guards. But getting out is going to require both your swimming skills and your wits. Because once you draw their attention away from my location, I'll be stranded in the water and an easy target if they see me and presume I'm escaping. Besides, the entire city is still looking for us, according to Sandeep."

"We'd lose the treasure *and* go to jail," Richard said. "I doubt Harvey would like that outcome."

"And neither would I," David said. "Let's go before the moon rises too high and causes us even more problems."

Richard and David crept up to the castle and used a small ledge for their footing to navigate around the perimeter to the more accessible area. When Richard surveyed the portal, he wasn't sure if the opening was created by a blast from a cannon or natural erosion over time. Either way, getting inside would've been relatively simple had one of the guards along the wall taken up a position above the section.

Richard picked up a large chunk of rock and hurled it out into the water, drawing the guard's attention away from the hole. Seizing their opportunity, Richard and David stole inside and initiated their search for the well. They followed

Sarita's detailed map and notes, leading them right to it. Per her advice, they stayed in the outer perimeter of the fortress, avoiding the people sequestered there.

Within ten minutes, they found the well just as Sarita had described it. David struck a match, revealing a board that covered the opening.

"This must be it," Richard said.

He and David worked quickly, setting aside the top. However, when they went to look inside, it was empty.

"I knew it," David growled. "She was playing us for fools this entire time. I'll bet she's on a train by now, laughing the entire way."

"That's one possible scenario," Richard said. "However, there could be another explanation."

David sighed before responding in a whisper. "When are you going to wake up and see the world for what it really is, Richard? How long is it going to take for you to recognize that the idea of people being inherently good is little more than a myth? Humans are rotten to the core."

Richard chuckled. "I guess I'll stop thinking that way when I'm convinced you're right about everyone. You've grown hardened after serving in the field of espionage. And a good spy always knows not everything is as it seems. How long will it take before you accept that fact?"

The clanking of metal against the stone floor arrested both Richard's and David's attention. They rushed toward the sound in the adjacent room. When they arrived there, an eerie stillness fell over the place.

"I thought she said no one came to this part of the castle," David said.

"Apparently, someone got curious."

"Too curious," David said with a growl.

Richard struck a match and glided around the wall,

inspecting it for any sign of other people. Just as he nearly completed his search, he heard another clanking noise, the sound of metals banging off stone. As Richard was drawn to the commotion, he struck another match and held it out in front of him. He gasped when the eyes of a man were illuminated in the darkness, revealing a disfigured face and one eye that had nearly lost all its color.

"Looking for this?" the man asked with a toothy grin.

Richard looked down at the man's hand and noticed a golden chalice.

"Give it to us now or else you will live to regret it," David said.

The old man snickered. "Keeping some of your stolen treasure would fall very low on my list of regrets. A simple glance at my face ought to tell you that much."

"As would hurting you fall on mine," David said.

"Gentlemen, there's no need to issue threats," Richard said. "I'm sure we can come to some sort of civil agreement."

"I keep this cup," the old man said. "You can have everything else."

Richard drew back and stared at the man. "*Everything?*"

"Just like that?" David asked, snapping his fingers for emphasis.

The old man nodded. "You obviously need it worse than I do. Besides, it doesn't matter how many riches you have if you're living in a leper colony. The government will seize all your possessions when you die, using it to pay for all the supplies and food as well as the guards' salaries who protect this place."

"They don't look like they're protecting you," David said. "More like they're protecting the rest of the city from you."

"You don't know them like we do," the old man said. "They're like family to us."

"Then why not give *them* the treasure?" Richard asked.

The old man smiled and shook his head. "Sometimes your family can be cruel." He pulled up his shirt to reveal a deep scar across his midsection.

"They did that to you?" Richard asked.

The old man nodded. "And they'll do it to you, too, if they catch you here. That much you can be sure of."

"Thank you," Richard said as he snatched up one of the sacks near the opening and twirled the burlap around to cinch it shut. David grabbed the other one, and the two men began the most harrowing portion of their mission: the exit.

Richard hustled toward a stairwell beneath the closest turret near the docked boat in the water. Working in tandem to repel down the pair of ropes positioned over the outside of the wall, Richard and David used one hand to grip the cord and the other to keep the jewels and coins from dropping into the water. Once they reached the boat, they secured the two sacks. David eased inside and wrapped his hands around the oars.

"On my signal," Richard said as he tossed David the rope that tethered the boat to the castle.

"And how will you let me know?" David asked.

"You'll know it when you hear it."

Richard climbed back up the fortress walls and slung himself onto the parapet when he was met by one of the guards.

"Hey," the guard said. "What are you doing here? You can't just enter this place like that."

Richard dusted his shirt off with both hands before acknowledging the man. "I'm sorry. I must've gotten turned around. Can you point me toward the nearest exit?"

"I'm no fool," the guard said as he pulled his sword out of its sheath. "I know who you are—and I'm going to run you through right now."

"You're going to regret that," Richard said.

"I doubt it," the guard said before launching into a sprint straight at Richard.

In a skillful move, he slid aside, avoiding the edge of the guard's blade. In the same motion, Richard threw his leg out, sending the guard tumbling to the ground. He came to a stop before lying still for a moment.

"Why don't you just forget you ever saw me and we'll call it a night?" Richard suggested.

"Only men who are losing offer to quit," the guard said as he rose to his feet.

"Help me out here, sir," Richard said. "I'm trying to save your life."

The guard growled as he made another run at Richard. But instead of resorting to the same tactic as the guard drew near, Richard dropped low before exploding upward and catching the man in the shoulder. The force knocked the guard off balance and into one of the embrasures in the crenelated wall. He absorbed the blow just above his knee, but the momentum of his upper body resulted in him careening over the edge.

Richard rushed to the side. The guard screamed as he plummeted onto the rocks near the foot of the fortress. Almost immediately, a murmur arose from the lepers as well as the other guard roaming around the parapet.

"Nigel," the other guard called. "Are you all right?"

The moonlight glistened on the water, and Richard realized if the guard looked over the edge, David would be exposed.

"Over here, you gutless coward," Richard shouted before breaking into a sprint in the opposite direction.

"Stop right there," the man yelled.

Richard didn't break his stride, continuing toward the

designated spot from which he wanted to dive. The other guard broke one way then back the other in an effort to take the shortest distance toward the intruder. While the way the man chose was what Richard wanted, it meant his margin for error was scant. Richard had surveyed the water, and the best location deep enough to handle a dive was about a hundred meters away. And the guard was equidistant from that spot as well.

Richard pumped his arms and stretched his legs with each stride. His lungs burned, and he struggled to breathe. A few seconds later, Richard honed in on the jumping location as the guard bore down. The two men continued on a collision course, and Richard could tell he needed to get creative to avoid getting apprehended or sliced by the guard's unsheathed sword.

With contact only seconds away, Richard leaped toward the inside portion of the wall and stepped up, propelling himself to the outer portion and into the lake. Richard tucked his legs and somersaulted twice before splashing down. When he surfaced, he heard the guard screaming at him from above.

Richard's arms sliced through the water, churning through it with desperate strokes. He wished he'd had time to strip down before diving over the ledge, but he embraced the challenge of swimming fully clothed, something he'd never done before on purpose.

After several minutes of hard swimming, Richard rolled onto his back and relaxed, catching his breath. He looked back at the leper colony, which was little more than a shadow in the pale moonlight. Then he flipped around and glanced at the shore. Headlights raced along the road that ran parallel to the shore.

Richard focused his efforts again and sliced through the water until it was shallow enough that he could scramble ashore. He found the clothes he'd left and changed quickly. He was already dressed and casually walking along the road when a car whizzed past, shining a spotlight onto the lake.

Despite his best efforts, Richard couldn't suppress a smile. He broke into a jog as he headed back toward the rendezvous point to meet up with David.

CHAPTER 32

Wilhelm stood back on the street with Reinhard, deferring to Ludwig to handle the initial confrontation. The man who'd reported the location of the woman's house to the Reichswehr unit chief watched from the side, demanding that Wilhelm issue immediate payment once the report was confirmed.

"Yes?" a woman said as she answered the door. "Do you realize what time of night it is?"

"Do you realize you are working with two wanted criminals?" Ludwig asked.

"What? I don't know what you're talking about. I—"

Ludwig stormed inside, pushing his way past her. Several other agents followed before Wilhelm and Reinhard joined the rest of the troops.

"You are Sarita, aren't you?" Wilhelm asked.

The woman stared at them wide-eyed with a furrowed brow. "Look, I don't know what you think I've done, but I'm—"

"Silence," Wilhelm shouted as he marched into the kitchen. "Lying will not help your situation. The two men you've been assisting took something of mine, and I want it back. If you want to get back to bed, I suggest you tell me where you hid them."

"Hid them?" she asked, scowling at Wilhelm as she followed him.

"That's right. The Americans! Where are they?"

"I'm afraid I don't know what you're talking about," she said. "I don't know any Americans. I'm going to have to ask you to leave now."

Wilhelm took his coat off and slung it around the back of a chair. He rolled up his sleeves, glaring at the woman.

"Sir, we've searched the house," Ludwig reported moments later. "We were unable to find anything."

Before Wilhelm could respond, a young girl waddled out into the hallway, squinting from the bright light emanating overhead.

"Mummy, I'm trying to go to sleep. What's going on?" she asked.

"Go back to bed, sweetie. I'll tuck you back in once everyone is gone in a couple minutes."

No one said a word until the girl disappeared down the hall into her room.

"I don't know what you think you're doing by charging into my house like this, but I'd like for you to leave right now before I summon a constable."

"You mean like this one?" Ludwig asked, pointing toward a British police officer standing behind several of the Reichswehr agents.

"I—I—what right do you have to barge in here like this?" she asked.

"We have every right when you're hiding American criminals. Now drop the act, and tell us the truth if you want to tuck your daughter back in bed. Where are they?"

"I already told you. I don't know what you're talking about."

Wilhelm gestured toward Ludwig. "Seize her. She's coming with us."

Sarita resisted the men, struggling to get free. But she relented when she realized it was all in vain.

Sarita's daughter had wandered back into the kitchen. "Mummy, where are they taking you?"

"Don't worry about me. Just go to bed. Your auntie will take care of you. I'm sure I'll be back in the morning."

"Don't count on it," Ludwig said before forcing her toward the door.

Wilhelm clapped his hands and then rubbed them together. "Finally, we're going to get some answers out of her."

* * *

THE REICHSWEHR TEAM WAS ALMOST OUT OF THE HOUSE when Reinhard glanced back one final time at the young girl. She heaved as tears rolled down her cheeks.

"Just a moment, sir," Reinhard said to Wilhelm before approaching Sarita's daughter.

Reinhard knelt next to her and offered her his handkerchief.

"Where are you taking my mummy?" she asked.

"We just need to talk to her and ask her a few questions. She'll be back before you know it, probably in time to make your breakfast in the morning. Is your aunt here now?"

The girl nodded. "She's asleep in my mother's room. She drinks a lot and doesn't wake up very easily."

"I'm sure she'll be able to take care of you in the morning. Now be a good little girl and run along to bed."

The girl scowled and stomped back to her room, slamming the door before breaking into another sobbing fit.

Reinhard sighed as he stood. He was about to leave when

he noticed Wilhelm's jacket still on the chair. Hustling over to fetch it, Reinhard noticed an envelope sticking out of the jacket's inside pocket. He glanced around to make sure he was still alone before inspecting the letter more closely. It was addressed to him and had been opened.

"What is this?" Reinhard asked.

He yanked out the folded paper and started reading. Moments later, he was sobbing.

"Are you coming?" Wilhelm called into the house.

Back to the door, Reinhard wiped away his tears and took a deep breath before responding. "Yes, sir. I'm on my way."

He discreetly reinserted the pages into the envelope before stuffing it back into the coat. Throwing it over his arm, he marched outside.

"Ah, my jacket," Wilhelm said. "I can't believe I almost left it."

"No worries, sir. It's been a long day."

"And it's going to be a long night, too, if this woman doesn't talk."

Reinhard thought about saying something but stopped. While he'd seen Wilhelm be nasty to people he didn't know, Reinhard couldn't fathom his boss would be so cruel to someone he did know.

CHAPTER 33

RICHARD HUSTLED OVER TO DAVID RECLINED AGAINST a tree on the opposite side of the shore. A warm breeze drifted across the lake and rustled the leaves overhead. David scrambled to his feet when Richard drew near.

"Thanks for the diversion," David said. "It's like I was rowing my boat gently down the stream."

"Well, you can thank my arms later," Richard said. "They feel like they're on fire."

"Are you ready to help me pull this cart another three miles?"

"Of course," Richard said. "The end of this operation is in sight. All we have to do is get up that ramp and into the fort."

"Easier said than done."

"Every part of our evening has fallen under that category. What's one more thing?"

David smiled. "So true. Let's get moving."

They each took up a position on the side of the rickshaw and pulled it behind them. Richard noted how it felt nearly effortless when someone else was helping him, even when the cart was weighed down with two bags full of treasure. They plodded along until they reached Sarita's house.

"If this idea of yours works, I'm going to recommend you get a promotion," David said.

Richard shrugged. "I don't care about that. I just want to see the world."

He walked around to the side of her house where several farm animals were sleeping peacefully for the night. Without wasting any time, he dug through the trough and found the small chest, roughly two feet square. A note was pinned on top along with a pair of gloves.

"That woman has saved our bacon twice now," David said. "Once more and we should nominate her for sainthood with the Pope."

"I thought you needed three miracles to be designated a saint?" Richard said.

"That's right—and it'll be a legitimate miracle if she helps us pull this off."

Richard reconfigured his sack, filling the box with a small handful of jewels and coins so he could fit the box inside one of the large burlap sacks.

Richard and David resumed their journey to Fort Jaigahr, remaining silent until they reached the bottom of the ramp.

"You got any strength left?" David asked.

Richard nodded. "Enough to get us to the top."

During his last attempt to get the treasure into the fortress, Richard had noted that workers lugged supplies up to the gates around 10:00 p.m. The steady stream gave Richard the idea that they could blend in, breaking away near the top and stealing around the side of the wall with their bags.

After waiting for a half hour, the caravan started right on time and the two Army Intelligence agents joined in, plodding their way toward the top. Twenty minutes later, they stopped as the rest of the workers reached the gate. Richard and

David slipped away into the shadows and navigated to the north side that wasn't guarded.

"Up for climbing another wall?" David asked.

Richard scowled. "What are we going to anchor the rope to?"

David didn't say a word as he dismantled the cart and attached one of the wheels to the end of a rope. He whirled it around before slinging it toward the parapet. The wheel crested the top of the wall and fell securely between one of the embrasures.

"It's sturdy," David said. "Want to give it a go?"

Richard nodded and then yanked on the rope. Satisfied that it was going to hold, he looped another rope around his belt and scurried to the top. Once there, he waited for David to affix a burlap bag loaded with treasure to the other end before hoisting it to the top. After both bags were safely atop the wall, David muscled his way up.

They crept along the parapet until they reached a stairwell and descended to ground level. After meandering along the walkway for a few minutes, Richard led David down another set of steps and into the bowels of the fortress. When they reached the room where all the water was stored, they used sticks and cloth they'd stuffed in their bags to form torches. Leading the way, Richard headed straight for the far right corner. After he laid his bag on the floor, he approached a portion of the wall that was cut out in an ornate fashion.

"How did you find this?" David asked.

"I saw it when we were looking for the treasure the first time, but I didn't have time to fully investigate it," Richard said as he felt around the space.

"Wait a second," David said. "You mean to tell me that you're going on a hunch right now?"

Richard nodded.

"I can't believe this. You told me you found a hiding place and—"

David's tirade was cut short as part of the wall slid to the side, revealing a small empty chamber. His mouth fell agape.

"How did you know?" David asked.

"Like I said, just a hunch. None of the other sections in the wall had this hidden lever, and I know from reading history that these rajas were all paranoid someone was going to take their treasure. And I bet this isn't the only room like this in the castle."

Richard and David emptied their sacks, spilling the treasure across the room. Once they were finished, Richard pocketed a couple coins before grabbing the chest and exiting the chamber. Once both agents were outside, David closed the secret door.

"You know the Hindus believe what you just did results in bad karma," David said.

"It's not for me," Richard said. "It's for my dad. He's got quite a coin collection, and I thought he might enjoy adding a couple of these to his stash. Besides, I don't believe in karma."

"Suit yourself," David said. "Just don't say I didn't warn you."

Richard strode to the designated holding tank and opened the chest. After reading the instructions in the note, he put on his gloves, drizzled the liquid from Sarita's vial over the jewels, and closed the box. Then he placed the box in the water, hiding the small chest well beneath the surface.

"I hope this works," David said.

Richard nodded confidently. "All we have to do now is get the Germans here."

"Is that all?" David asked with a sigh. "I can't wait for this operation to be over."

They hustled upstairs and looked for the gates. Just as they were about to walk into the courtyard, Richard stopped and put his hand on David's chest.

"Look," Richard whispered. "Reichswehr soldiers."

Four Germans working in pairs were questioning the people who had brought up supplies earlier that evening.

"I thought you told Sandeep not to send the Germans here until after midnight?" David asked.

"I did," Richard said. "But something must've happened. They're not going to stop until they're convinced there's nothing to look for."

"Or we're dead," David added.

"Yes, there's that too."

"We need to sit tight."

"I agree," Richard said. "If we have a front row seat for the show, at least we'll know if it's really going to be over."

"Should we return to the bowels of this place?" David asked.

Richard nodded. "But let's stay in the shadows."

They crept along, crouching low to avoid detection. However, when they were about halfway to the passageway, a little girl darted in front of them.

"Hello," she said.

Richard froze. He glanced over at David, who was staring wide-eyed at her.

"Hello," Richard said softly as he bent over to get eye level with her. "What's your name?"

"Indira Nehru," she said confidently.

"And what are you doing here all alone, Indira?" Richard asked.

"My father is here on business, and I'm exploring the fort."

"At this time of night?" Richard asked.

"Are you the ones they're looking for?" she asked.

"Who's looking for someone?"

"Over there," she said, pointing toward the soldiers. "Those men are looking for someone. Is it you?"

"They are," Richard said. "But we didn't do anything wrong."

"I'm not sure I believe you."

Richard cut his eyes over at David, but he was surveying the activity across the fort. "Why don't you help us out—and we'll help you out? Sound good to you?"

She shrugged. "I guess so."

"Good," Richard said. "When they ask you if you saw us, tell them you've been all over the fort and you didn't see anything."

"But that's a lie," she said.

"It might be a little one, but those men are going to hurt us, and we didn't do anything to them," Richard said. "At least anything they didn't deserve."

"And how are you going to help me?" she asked.

"I'm going to tell you where a great treasure is."

Her eyes lit up. "A treasure? Here?"

Richard put his finger to his lips. "I'll tell you everything, but first you have to tell the soldiers that you didn't see anything when they ask. Understand?"

She nodded and smiled. "I like you. You seem like a nice man."

"I like you too, Indira. Now hurry along."

Richard watched her race across the courtyard and engage the Reichswehr operatives in conversation. After she finished talking, one of the agents called for the others and they exited the fort.

Richard sighed and slumped against the wall.

"At least they're gone," David said. "Though you had to

lie to a little girl."

"Who said I was lying?" Richard said.

"You're going to tell her where the treasure is?" David asked as he chuckled. "Look, I'm not complaining. The Germans are gone, but you had to lie to her to make them go away."

"Just forget about it," Richard said. "Let's get downstairs and sit tight. We're almost home free. All we have to do now is wait for the Germans to come back."

CHAPTER 34

WILHELM EYED HIS SOLDIERS AND CONSIDERED THE information they'd just delivered. He paced around the pub, throwing back the rest of his drink before slamming his glass down on the bar.

"So, let me see if I understand this," Wilhelm said. "You scoured the fort and didn't see them but just decided to come back and report this to me?"

The soldiers nodded.

"We searched everywhere, and they're not there," one of the men said.

"I told you not to come back until you found them," Wilhelm said. "I know they're still there, lurking in the shadows and laughing at you fools." He grunted and gestured for another drink. "It seems like my *wolfsrudel* has been defanged by these young Americans."

Reinhard, who had been outside, strode in with a familiar man. "Sir, I have some other news for you."

Wilhelm grunted and took another swig of his drink. "What is it now?"

"Do you remember Sandeep?" Reinhard asked.

"The man who threw us into this state of disarray?" Wilhelm asked. "How could I forget him?"

"He has something to tell you," Reinhard said.

"Out with it," Wilhelm said with a growl.

"I know where the treasure is," Sandeep said.

"And how do you know this?" Wilhelm demanded.

Sandeep took a deep breath. "Because I overheard the two Americans talking tonight as they were sneaking through the city. They were pulling a cart that had a blanket thrown over the top."

"It's got to be the treasure, sir," Ludwig said.

"And you're certain they're there now?" Wilhelm asked Sandeep.

He nodded. "I watched them take the long winding path, merging into a line with all the other men taking supplies to Fort Jaigahr."

Wilhelm poured some tobacco into his pipe and lit it. "Yet my men were just there and they found nothing."

"With all due respect, sir, perhaps they should search again. I know what I saw."

"Very well then," Wilhelm said before turning to Ludwig. "Get the woman and bring him too. We need to get moving."

* * *

A HALF HOUR LATER, WILHELM TRUDGED UP THE HILL WITH the rest of his men as well as Sandeep and Sarita. Neither one of them said a word as they followed Wilhelm's men. After talking their way inside the gates, Wilhelm asked Sandeep to lead them to the object that the Americans were hiding.

"How do we know this isn't a trap, sir?" Reinhard asked.

"We don't," Wilhelm said. "But we do know that there are only two of them and a dozen of us. You should appreciate those odds."

Once they reached the center of the courtyard, the men fanned out, forming three teams of four soldiers each.

"This isn't necessary," Sandeep said. "I know where they planned to hide the treasure."

Wilhelm shook his head and wagged his finger at Sandeep. "You don't know what is necessary and what isn't in the frontlines of war. You must take precautions to make sure your enemies aren't planning to ambush you."

The search lasted for an hour without anything of significance being found.

"Happy now?" Sandeep asked.

"You can never be too cautious," Wilhelm warned. "Now, where is that treasure?"

"Follow me," Sandeep said.

With all the troops reunited in the main courtyard, Sandeep walked briskly toward a stairwell and then descended to the lower level. He led them to the room full of cisterns and came to a stop next to one labeled number nine.

"It's in here," Sandeep said as he pointed to the water and then took a step back.

"Fetch it for us then," Wilhelm said.

Sandeep hesitated before he glanced at Sarita. She gave him an approving nod. He dipped his hands into the water and moved them around. After a few seconds, he hoisted a small chest to the surface.

Wilhelm scowled. "That can't be all. I know there was more than that."

"They said they were going to hide everything in the castle after they spread some of the wealth throughout the city," Sandeep said.

"That's why no one has come forward with information about their whereabouts," Wilhelm said, shaking his fist angrily. "They're bribing the people."

Sandeep nodded. "I'd much rather get a reward of five hundred pounds than a worthless artifact."

Wilhelm smiled. "Well, these artifacts are far from worthless. In fact, they're quite priceless."

He knelt next to the chest and prepared to open it.

"No!" shouted Sarita. "Don't open it. That chest is cursed."

Wilhelm glared back at her. "What is it this time? Some silly Hindu belief of yours?"

"There's a symbol etched on the top," she said, her hands quaking. "If you remove anything from that chest, you will die."

Wilhelm sighed as he staggered to his feet. "Klaus, Hans, please come here and show this woman that there's nothing to be afraid of."

The two Reichswehr agents walked up to the chest and hunched over it. Klaus lifted the lid, while Hans plunged his hands inside to pick up some of the jewels. He held them out for Wilhelm to see and then Sarita.

"See," Wilhelm said. "Your tales of superstition are nothing more than—"

Hans crumpled to the floor and started to shake. The jewels bounced on the stone, scattering in every direction.

"It's cursed, I tell you," Sarita said, her voice trembling. "If we don't get out of here now, we might all end up dead."

Klaus laughed. "Come on, Hans. That isn't funny."

"He's not joking," Sarita said. "He was struck down for trying to steal from that chest. And if any of you dare try it as well, you will suffer the same fate."

Wilhelm eyed her closely. "Your magic tricks won't work on us. Klaus, grab some of the gold and give Sarita a piece."

Klaus hesitated.

"Do it now!" Wilhelm roared.

Klaus's hands shook as he reached inside to retrieve a few pieces of the treasure. However, as he turned around to present the handful of riches to Sarita, he collapsed and began convulsing on the floor.

"Why don't you believe me?" Sarita asked. "We're all going to die."

Wilhelm stamped his foot. "I don't know how you're doing this, but I'm not going to stand by and watch you make fools of us all. Now, *you* come over here and pull out a few pieces of gold."

Sarita shook her head and walked backward. "It's cursed. I can't do it."

"Oh, yes, you can," Wilhelm sneered as he grabbed her by her arm. "And you will."

CHAPTER 35

Richard had enjoyed watching the Reichswehr soldiers fall the moment they touched the treasure, but Wilhelm's sudden demand that Sarita retrieve a piece of gold changed that. Richard's mood went from satisfaction to sheer terror. If Wilhelm discovered the seizures were being induced by a poison Sarita concocted, he would likely kill her and figure out another way to extra the fortune from the box.

"We can't let her do that," Richard whispered as he turned toward David. "They'll figure it out and make off with the loot, not to mention probably kill Sarita on their way out."

"I agree, but what can we do about it?" David asked. "We can't do anything without costing us our lives."

Richard shrugged. "I'm going in to help her."

"You can't do that," David said, grabbing hold of Richard's arm. "That'd be suicide."

Richard ripped his arm away from David and glared at him. "I'll be fine."

"I'm not going to feel bad about leaving you if you do something this stupid," David said.

"There's nothing stupid about what I'm going to do. But I still need your help."

"Wait, let's think about this."

"There's nothing to think about. All I need you to do is create a diversion."

"And when do you want me to do that?" David asked.

"You'll know when. Just watch."

Richard eased onto the floor and walked into the illuminated portion of the room where everyone could see him. He raised both hands in the air.

"I'll do it," Richard said.

The remaining Reichswehr operatives swung around in his direction, training their weapons on Richard.

"You'll do what, Mr. Halliburton?" Wilhelm asked.

"I'll fetch the treasure for you."

"I should have you shot right now," Wilhelm said. "We'd be long gone by now if it weren't for your constant meddling in our affairs."

"You mean your thievery of ancient artifacts?"

Wilhelm grunted. "Maybe I will just shoot you right here. At least I wouldn't have to worry about you ever again."

Richard shrugged. "You could, but do you really want to do that when none of your men have the courage to remove the massive fortune inside that chest? Now that I think about it, I didn't see you volunteering either."

"Empty the treasure into that sack now," Wilhelm said. "And when you're done, you can show me where the rest of the jewels and coins are."

"Everything that's valuable is in that chest. All the other items were meaningful to archeologists but not worth much."

"So you know the secret to removing objects from that chest?" Wilhelm said.

"I hope so," Richard said. "I never took anything out. I only put things in it."

"And here you are, riding in at the last moment like the chivalrous knight to save the damsel in distress," Wilhelm said. "Something seems amiss to me."

"What can I say," Richard said. "You trapped me inside when you entered the room, and I had nowhere else to go."

Wilhelm chuckled as he circled around the chest. "I have to admit that attempting to hide the treasure back here was rather clever. But never underestimate the power of a bounty."

"Or the greed of human nature," Richard said.

"Enough," Wilhelm said with a growl as he kicked the sack toward Richard. "Empty the treasure in here now."

Richard took a deep breath and plunged his hand into the chest. Opening his palm, he revealed a pair of coins."See," he said with a wide grin. "There was nothing to be afraid of."

Before Richard could say another word, he fell onto the ground and started convulsing and seizing.

* * *

DAVID WATCHED FROM THE SHADOWS, WAITING FOR THE right moment to create a diversion. With Sarita in danger, he knew he couldn't wait much longer before taking action.

Damn you, Richard.

"It's cursed, I tell you," Sarita said again. "I warned you all, but no one would listen to me."

Wilhelm spun toward her. "I'm willing to sacrifice one more person to prove your theory right—*you*."

"No, I can't. I don't want to die."

Wilhelm grabbed her by the arm and dragged her toward the box. Then he cocked his pistol and held it to her head.

"Please, don't kill me. I have a daughter at home who needs me."

Wilhelm grabbed her by her hair and put his mouth next to her ear. "Empty the chest," he growled.

Reinhard stepped forward. "Sir, is this really necessary? Why don't we just take the box and figure this out later? We don't need to make any orphans tonight."

Wilhelm glanced at Reinhard. "Since when did you become concerned about orphans?"

"Since I know my children are now just a heartbeat away from becoming orphans themselves."

Wilhelm studied Reinhard. "You know then?"

Reinhard nodded. "The letter fell out of your coat pocket, the letter addressed to me. How could you keep that from me?"

"I was trying to keep you focused," Wilhelm said. "The future of our nation should be more important to you than ever now that your wife is gone."

"That's not how a good leader behaves."

"We'll finish this later," Wilhelm said, trying to hold Sarita still as she squirmed in his grasp.

"No, we're going to finish this right now," Reinhard said, raising his weapon and training it on Wilhelm. "*You* are going to empty that chest."

"This is not the time to challenge my authority," Wilhelm said, grabbing Sarita and holding her in front of him. "This woman is going to empty the treasure for us, and you're going to stand down."

Wilhelm held Sarita's right arm and forced it toward the chest.

David figured that was his cue and started screaming and yelling from the darkness. The commotion made all the Reichswehr agents, including Wilhelm, freeze as they looked in David's direction to figure out what was happening.

At that moment, Richard rolled over and snapped the

box shot. Then he kicked Wilhelm in the chest, freeing Sarita. Richard grabbed her wrist and pulled her with him as they vanished into the darkness.

A pair of shots rang out before the members of the Reichswehr unit went scrambling after them.

"That was quite the performance," David said as they ran. "You had me fooled there for a minute."

Richard relinquished his grip on Sarita and hugged the box against his chest. "Take her out of here, and get her some place safe."

"What are you going to do?"

"I'll think of something. Now go."

CHAPTER 36

RICHARD OFTEN WONDERED IF HE'D EVER TIRE OF flirting with danger, a temptress whose appeal was cloaked in a rush unlike any other human experience. However, he never raised such questions during those times when he was enraptured by her beauty. Instead, he preferred to drink in the moment. And getting chased by ten Reichswehr troops through an Indian fortress at night while toting a treasure chest was a sadistic thrill, sending endorphins coursing through his veins.

Despite his unmitigated joy, Richard's legs burned as he raced along the breezeways, illuminated only by the pale moonlight overhead. He sucked in another breath while scanning the next path he wanted to take. The Germans were gaining on him, though he'd managed to dash around a corner and leave them guessing as to which way he went.

Two bullets whizzed past his head, alerting him to the fact that he was no longer out of sight. The operatives were closing fast, and he needed to do something to get away.

The gunshots echoed off the walls, sending the British security guards scrambling to the center of the fortress to investigate. Richard darted around the corner and raced toward the holding pond that was about one hundred yards square. After one deep breath, he dove into the water, clutching the chest. He came up for air and took note of his location before letting go of the box and plunging underneath the water again. Despite staying submerged, a couple bullets hit nearby.

Richard strained as he stroked his way to the other side. About halfway across, he felt the urge to take a breath. But he resisted, knowing that the Reichswehr agents were just waiting to fire at him. Meanwhile, voices shouted above. He couldn't determine what was being said, but he could sense the anger in those words.

After about a minute, Richard thrust his hand out in front of him, contacting the wall. He paused before bobbing to the surface and quickly tried to ascertain the situation.

British security personnel stood at the edge above and yelled across the water. On the other three sides, Reichswehr agents all had their weapons trained on Richard.

"Those men are trying to kill me," Richard said before ducking down.

He waited a few more seconds to determine if the agents were going to start shooting at his location. When he figured out that they weren't, he eased back up and glanced around. The Germans were gone.

"What did you do?" one of the guards asked.

"Those men are German soldiers operating illegally outside the Treaty of Versailles," Richard said as he wiped water away from his face. "They were trying to steal an ancient treasure hidden in this fortress."

"And you stopped them—all on your own?"

"I had some help," Richard said. "A lot actually. But you can't let them get away with this."

The guard gestured toward the other nearby men, who broke into pursuit of the Reichswehr troops.

"And where's this treasure now?" he asked.

"I'll get it for you," Richard said.

Richard climbed out and walked around the edge to the spot where he was certain he had dropped the treasure. He returned to the location and dove to the bottom. After remaining underwater for a few minutes, he resurfaced with a scowl on his face.

"That's odd," Richard said while treading water.

"What is it?" asked the guard.

"The treasure chest—it's gone."

CHAPTER 37

WILHELM SLUMPED TO THE FLOOR, HIS BACK TO THE door. Scattered around the room, all of his agents who'd survived were crouched low. They won a race to the market and all circled back to their temporary headquarters while operating out of Jaipur. The Fort Jaigahr guards and several other constables aroused to look for the German troops had called off their search for the night as evidenced by the hush that had fallen over the city several hours ago.

But Wilhelm had remained wide-eyed in the darkness, unable to sleep for more than a few minutes at a time as he pondered how they would escape not only the situation but also the country. Possessing official papers to move about the country was free of trouble as long as they abided by the rules. However, a rule had been broken when Wilhelm's obsession over the treasure superseded his own wisdom when it came to working on foreign soil. Now, the Reichswehr agents needed to figure a way out.

A rooster crowed as daylight broke, arousing several of the men, including Reinhard. Wilhelm wasn't sure what to do with his top lieutenant who, despite being irate over the letter incident, was still with the troops.

"We're going to get out of this," Wilhelm said.

"We have to," Reinhard said. "My children need a father."

"I'm sorry about Annemarie. She was a good woman. And I'm sorry that I kept that news from you. It was selfish of me. The truth is as much as I believe in this group of warriors, I don't trust anyone as much as I trust you."

"I'm a soldier, sir. We're trained to handle despairing news in the midst of battle. I wouldn't have lost my focus."

Wilhelm sighed, pausing before he spoke. "Being trained for something like that and actually experiencing it are entirely different matters. It's your loved ones who you think might have to handle dealing with a message about your death. But the other way around? Never. And that's why it's so difficult on us while we're out here trying to make the world safe for those back home."

"My situation is far more difficult," Reinhard said. "I lost my wife and my children lost their mother, a woman my youngest will never know. I can't stay out here without knowing that they're going to be taken care of."

"They are," Wilhelm said. "I asked for Annemarie's father, General Hindenburg, to make sure they're properly looked after. Your eldest daughter will be in the finest school in Berlin, and your new daughter will be have the opportunity to be watched by the nanny who helped raise your wife."

Reinhard shook his head. "I take it this means you're keeping me here."

Wilhelm sighed. "I wanted to send you back home to accompany the treasure, but that chance ended at the castle. If only you'd let that woman retrieve all the gold from that chest."

"Are you blaming me now?" Reinhard asked, clenching his fists. "I've done nothing but be loyal to you as you've led us to foreign countries, and this is the way you repay me, by making me stay and keeping me from grieving my wife's death?"

"We have one more opportunity before our entire unit returns home," Wilhelm said. "I promise."

"Where?" Reinhard asked.

"China. It's an artifact so rare that if we find it, we might be able to raise more than enough to rebuild our military from scratch."

"That's farther from home."

Wilhelm nodded. "It's our only way home. General Seeckt expects us to return with the raja's lost treasure."

"Then what will you do?"

"I'll stall," Wilhelm said. "I'll lie and tell him we have it but we must first go to China before we miss out on our chance there. It'll give us the opportunity to return to Germany as heroes. Seeckt will forget about our failure here if he can rebuild the military."

Reinhard nodded. "And if we fail in China?"

"We'll all be orphaning our children."

"There's just one problem," Reinhard said.

"What's that?"

"We still have to get out of Jaipur."

Wilhelm smiled. "I have a plan."

As sunlight started to stream through the windows, voices in the distance echoed in the streets. Wilhelm scrambled to his feet and told the soldiers awake to get everyone up.

"It's time to move," Wilhelm said. "Everybody out."

The Reichswehr unit went outside where Wilhelm gave Reinhard a new set of orders.

"Take everyone just past the train station," Wilhelm said. "I know they'll be looking for us there, but I'm going to divert the authorities so that they all look in a different place."

"How are you going to do that?"

"Leave that up to me. Hurry before they get here."

Wilhelm watched his men scatter into the streets until they were gone. Then he hustled to the market and found Manish brewing up an early morning batch of curry. He was dumping spices into a large pot when he looked up and recognized Wilhelm.

"You finally came for my curry," Manish said.

"Not exactly," Wilhelm said. "I wanted to see if you wanted to make five hundred pounds."

Manish was tasting his concoction when he slowly pulled the spoon away from his lips. "Did you say five hundred pounds?"

Wilhelm nodded. "I need you to divert the British soldiers who are looking for me and my men."

Manish sighed. "The hunter has become the hunted."

"Unfortunately, that's the case. So, will you help me?"

Manish shrugged. "For five hundred pounds, I'll do that and make you curry every day for an entire year."

"Good. Here's what I need you to do. Go to the police station and report that you saw the German men heading toward Fort Jaigahr and overhead us saying something about the treasure. And then go buy every seat in the final carriage of this morning's train. There should be enough to cover the cost and pay you your handsome fee."

"That's it?"

Wilhelm nodded as he handed Manish a small envelope stuffed with cash. "Don't let me down."

Manish stuffed the envelope into the back of his pants and darted from behind his kiosk in the direction of the nearest police station.

* * *

An hour later, Wilhelm reunited with the rest of the Reichswehr troops a mile on the outskirts of Jaipur along the railroad tracks. In the distance, the brakes hissed followed by the slow chugging of the wheels as the 8:00 a.m. train departed the station.

"Did it work?" Reinhard asked.

"We'll soon find out." Wilhelm paused as he maintained his gaze toward the oncoming locomotive. "I'm sorry about Annemarie, and I'm sorry I kept that information from you. I thought I was doing the right thing."

Reinhard stared off in the distance. "It doesn't matter now. Being angry at you won't bring her back. I need to move on and trust that General Hindenburg is providing my children with the care they need. But you know what the worst part is?"

"What?"

"We didn't even have names picked out yet for a girl."

"I would suggest you name her Annemarie after her mother. She was a good woman."

A couple minutes later, the train came into view and was still building up steam.

"Get ready," Wilhelm said.

As the train approached their position, the Reichswehr agents darted out of the tree line one by one and filed into the final car, which was completely empty.

"It worked," Wilhelm said as he sat down next to Reinhard, who cracked a faint smile.

Wilhelm stood and paced up and down the aisle, contemplating what to say as they left Jaipur behind. He finally turned around and addressed his *wolfsrudel.*

"We leave this place today with great disappointment that we were unable to fulfill our objectives, but our mission is still very much alive," Wilhelm said. "We will find what we're looking for in China. And we will restore our country's military to be the greatest the world has ever seen."

The men broke into applause as Wilhelm sat down. He wasn't happy about what had happened, but he certainly wasn't about to accept defeat.

CHAPTER 38

RICHARD SPENT THE NIGHT IN A JAIL CELL AT THE Jaipur police station. His arrest wasn't one he entirely objected to since Wilhelm's men were still on the loose. While the Reichswehr unit had acted brazenly in the past, Richard couldn't imagine a scenario where they would attempt to kill him while in police custody.

Just as the sun beamed through the windows, Richard was awakened by the jangling of keys and the creak of his cell door swinging open.

"You have a visitor, Mr. Halliburton," a constable said.

Richard sprang to his feet once he saw David. "You made it. Thank God. And Sarita?"

"She's safe along with her daughter."

"I knew you would figure out the right time to create a diversion."

David rubbed his forehead. "You almost got us both killed last night."

"But I didn't, " Richard said before leaning in close and continuing in a whisper, "and the Germans don't have the treasure."

"So who has the chest?" David asked in a hushed tone.

"It's still in the retention pond. Think you can get back there tonight to get it?"

"Are you kidding me?"

Richard shook his head. "No, I'm dead serious. I have no idea how long I'm going to be in here, and I need your help."

"Fine. Tell me where it is, and I'll go back tonight."

Richard smiled. "Just don't get caught, okay?"

After Richard explained where the treasure was, he promised to meet up at Sarita's house later that night.

"Good luck," Richard said before David left, who turned and gave a dismissive wave as he exited the cell.

A half an hour passed, and Richard was called upon again.

"Mr. Richard Halliburton?" asked a uniformed man lumbering across the floor.

"Yes," Richard said as he rose to his feet.

"I'm Arthur Pellman, the chief constable here. I understand you had quite an evening."

"Yes, sir."

Pellman gestured for Richard to exit the cell. "Why don't you come tell me about it?"

Richard settled into a chair across from Pellman's desk and recounted all of the evening's events, including his race through the fort to elude capture by the Germans.

"I was under the impression that they were here legally," Pellman said.

"That's what Alex Fullerton wanted you to believe. Is he still in Jaipur?"

"I believe so. He levied some serious accusations against you on a recent excursion to Maredumilli."

Richard shook his head resolutely. "Those are all lies, sir. He had someone plant evidence on us. There's no way we could've taken anything from his office without him seeing it since we were in his presence the entire time, not to mention the fact that we left our bags inside while we walked around the village with him. He's the reason the Germans were able to move so freely around the country when they should've never obtained the proper documents to do so in the first place."

Pellman stroked his chin and nodded. "I see."

Richard strained to see the notes written on a sheet of paper in front of Pellman. When he noticed Richard's wandering eyes, the chief constable repositioned the folder, holding it upright and closer to his vest.

"So, what exactly were you doing here in Jaipur?" Pellman asked.

"Preventing that group of elite German soldiers from getting their hands on those ancient artifacts."

"And that serves the U.S. interests in what way?"

Richard sighed and shook his head. "Sometimes, we don't just do things for our own interests, but also for the interests of others."

"So you spent your time reading the book of Philippians, did you?"

Richard chuckled. "I see you have a keen grasp of scripture. The Apostle Paul's words are as true for us individually as they are for us as a nation."

Pellman grunted. "That's rich coming from an American."

"Let's not be petty about this, sir. I can assure you that I'm neither a treasure hunter nor a thief."

"If you're a treasure hunter, you're a lousy one, that's for sure. But I'm not so sure that you aren't a thief. I'm willing to render a judgment on you right now that will get you out of Jaipur after spending three days in jail."

Richard moaned. "Sir, with all due respect, I've spent more days in prison already to last me a lifetime. How about you do the right thing and drop all charges before I contact the U.S. Embassy to get involved in a case that will expose British government corruption in one of the queen's beloved colonies?"

Pellman stared at the ceiling for a moment. "Fine—on one condition."

"Name it."

"That you leave Jaipur on the first train in the morning and never return."

"I'll accept those terms," Richard said. "Just draw up the official documents so I can sign them, and I'll be on my way."

Once Richard received his official release, it was sometime after noon. He headed to Sandeep's house to thank him for his help. Sandeep, in turn, served Richard a lavish lunch filled with all of India's finest delicatessens, including gajar ka halwa and brijal bharta. After gorging himself, Richard spent a few minutes playing with Smita while Sandeep showed off his snake charming prowess.

"You're getting better," Richard said, "both your musical skills and your ability to keep the snakes following you. Perhaps you have a future as a street performer."

Sandeep smiled. "I am glad we crossed paths, Mr. Halliburton. Jaipur will never be the same without you. Maybe you will write about us in one of your books?"

Richard shrugged. "It's possible, yet this might be a tale I omit."

* * *

AFTER SENDING HANK FOSTER A TELEGRAPH EXPLAINING the outcome of the mission, Richard sauntered over to Sarita's house. He entertained her daughter for an hour before bedtime, telling her stories of adventure at sea, some of them true, some of them creatively re-imagined. Once she had fallen asleep, he tucked her in and joined Sarita outside on the front porch steps, illuminated only by candlelight.

"You have a beautiful daughter," Richard said.

Sarita smiled and patted Richard's hand. "And thanks to you and David, she still has a mother."

He thanked her for her assistance in scaring off the Germans with her potion that caused seizures.

"You wouldn't have died if you'd touched the liquid," she said.

"I know," he said, "but the Germans weren't sure of anything. It's why they shot two of their own before they came after us. They wanted to make sure there were no soldiers left behind to confess the truth about what they were doing in India, even though it's obvious now."

"Do you think anyone will try to stop them?" she asked.

"I'm not sure anyone else would believe the Germans have the bravado to do something so brash after living under the burden of a crushing post-war treaty. But there are a few officers in the U.S. Army Intelligence who believe the worst about the Reichswehr's capabilities. And that's why I'm here."

The sound of footsteps in the dark startled Richard. He eased in front of Sarita, shielding her from any potential danger.

"It's just me," David said as he lugged the chest on his shoulder.

"You found it," she said.

Richard nodded. "And it's all yours."

She looked at him wide-eyed. "You can't be serious?"

"A promise is a promise," Richard.

"Oh, thank you," she said, grabbing Richard and hugging him.

David sighed. "Yeah, don't mind me. I'm just shivering

from walking back from the fort while sopping wet. Forget that I was the one who went back and got the chest for you."

Sarita lunged at David and hugged him too. She laughed once she backed away from him, looking down at her clothes to realize she was also wet now.

"I warned you," David said.

"I don't care," Sarita said, her toothy smile nearly overpowering the faint light.

"A deal is a deal," Richard said. "And all that we ask now is that you make a better life for you and your daughter. Think you can do that for us?"

Sarita nodded. "I think I can."

* * *

RICHARD AND DAVID TOOK THE FIRST TRAIN OUT OF JAIPUR the next morning, riding it straight through the night to Calcutta. When they arrived at the station, Harvey Carrington greeted them and led them to his car.

"Where are we going?" Richard asked.

"Someone wants to meet with you."

Twenty minutes later, they were walking across the balcony of a hotel overlooking the water. Hank Foster leaned against the railing with his arms crossed and a wide grin across his face.

"I sure am glad I was right about you," Hank said.

"I'm only alive because of your friend Dr. Knapp. He taught me a thing or two in the jungle."

"Well, I wanted to thank you for your service on these past two missions," Hank said. "From what I've gathered based on your report, this wasn't an easy assignment."

David chuckled. "This is Captain Make It More Difficult

right here. If there's an easy way to do something, Richard will ignore it and find a more challenging approach."

"We're alive, aren't we?" Richard asked with a wry smile.

"And the Germans don't have possession of the treasure," Hank said. "That was the original mission, too. By the way, where is it?"

"Where's what?" Richard asked.

"Where's the treasure?"

Richard shrugged. "It was the strangest thing because it suddenly went missing."

Hank threw his hands in the air. "Whatever, I don't care. As long as the Reichswehr didn't get its grimy little hands on it, it doesn't matter to me. The mission was a success, and I'll make sure you both receive commendations for your work in India."

"Thank you, sir," Richard said. "It was our pleasure to serve."

Hank sighed. "Speaking of which, I have another assignment for you, if you're interested."

"Oh?" Richard said as his eyebrows shot upward. "Where are the Germans headed next?"

"China," Hank said. "They're looking for an ancient seal that's worth millions."

Richard shrugged. "Count me in. I've always wanted to go to China."

EPILOGUE

August 5, 1976
Jaipur, India

INDIRA GHANDI PACED AROUND THE COURTYARD OF THE ancient Fort Jaigahr. The compound was just as she had remembered it, though somewhat more dilapidated. The warm breeze whipping through the fort made her smile and think back to a time when life was much simpler.

She looked down at the letter in her hand, one postmarked from November 1939. The letter, however, was written nearly a year earlier. She wasn't sure why there was such a discrepancy in the dates, but it was significant, catching her attention almost immediately.

The envelope was addressed to Indira Nehu. She hadn't been called that in years, not since she forsook her father's name after marrying Feroze, who'd long since widowed her. She removed the paper and read it once more:

April 5, 1938

Dear Indira,

You may not remember me, but I remember you. Your sweet face and willingness to help out a stranger in need is something I've never forgotten.

I'm not sure when you'll receive this—or if you'll receive it all. But I wanted to send you a map. If you remember where we met, you'll know the location and be able to follow this to a vast treasure.

You may wonder why I'm sending this to you right now all these years later, but it's because there are some things you do in life that you wish you could change. And one of my longtime regrets is that I didn't make sure the people of India were able to enjoy the vast treasure that belonged to them. I trust you'll retrieve this fortune and handle it with care.

Warmest regards,
Richard Halliburton

Indira Ghandi had shut down the area around Fort Jaigahr for three days. Outside the walls, journalists and citizens alike buzzed with what was going on inside. For centuries, the tale of a hidden treasure in the fortress had ascended to legendary status in Indian culture. And if there was ever a time that India needed financial help, it was in the middle of an emergency declared by Indira, the country's prime minister.

Indira had almost forgotten about the letter until a month earlier when she found it while rummaging through some old boxes in her basement. Initially, the note sounded strange, like it was intended for someone else. But she was going through some official documents of her father's and found a report dated from 1922 where he mentioned that he took her on a trip to Jaipur. And suddenly, the memory rushed back. She could still see the handsome foreigner pleading with her not to let anyone know she had seen him. There was something about him that made her believe he was a trustworthy man.

"Prime Minister," a soldier shouted from across the courtyard. "We've located it. Please come with me."

Indira strode through the walkways of the fortress and descended into the bowels, upon which she saw a light glowing in the corner. When she approached it, she found soldiers crammed into a room and huddled over a vast fortune.

She gasped with wide eyes and mouth agape. "I never thought it was true."

"It's true," one of the soldiers exclaimed. "And I don't believe it myself either."

Indira smiled. "Box it up," she said, "and not a word of this to anyone. It'd be a shame to ruin one of our country's greatest legends."

THE END

ACKNOWLEDGMENTS

THIS PROJECT HAS BEEN INCREDIBLY EXCITING AND fun to embark upon, mixing fiction with fact. And quite frankly, none of it would've ever come about without my wife's introduction of Richard Halliburton to me through his timeless Book of Marvels. My children also played a huge role in convincing me to write something about Halliburton after they read his books and would regale me with his stories everyday until I finally decided I needed to read them for myself.

I'd like to thank Rhodes College and Bill Short for allowing me access to Richard Halliburton's archived journals and other material that helped fill in the blanks about what kind of man Richard really was and where he really went. Bill was an incredible help in gathering the information for me and graciously allowing me to plod my way through the material I requested. Without Bill's assistance, I'm not sure this project would've ever become a reality—at least in my lifetime.

And a big thank you to Muan Songput for visiting Jaipur and getting video to help me have a more accurate depiction of the city.

And as always, this book wouldn't be what it is without Krystal Wade's skillful editorial direction. She made this book much better than when I originally conceived it.

And last but certainly not least, I'm most grateful for you, the reader, who decided to invest your time with one of my stories. I hope you had as much fun reading this book as I did writing it.